THE
UNTARNISHED
BADGE

Other Books by S. J. Stewart

THE
UNTARNISHED
BADGE

•

S. J. Stewart

AVALON BOOKS
NEW YORK

Published by Avalon Books,
an imprint of Thomas Bouregy & Co., Inc.
New York, NY

Library of Congress Cataloging-in-Publication Data

Stewart, S. J.
    The untarnished badge / S. J. Stewart.
        p.   cm.
    ISBN 978-0-8034-7466-6 (hardcover : acid free paper)
    I. Title.
    PS3569.T473U58   2012
    813'.54—dc23

                                            2011033932

PRINTED IN THE UNITED STATES OF AMERICA
ON ACID-FREE PAPER
BY RR DONNELLEY, HARRISONBURG, VIRGINIA

Dedicated to Jason H. Stewart
for his computer know-how and
for his unfailing kindness

Chapter One

Late-afternoon shadows were lengthening as Luke Cochran rode into the frontier town of Braxton. The place had the look of any typical frontier settlement that had been built in anticipation of the railroad. The builders had been disappointed though, for the rails were laid elsewhere. Still the town survived. There were nearby cattle ranches, and Braxton was a place to buy the necessities, visit friends, go to church, or enjoy the hospitality of a saloon. And the rails that had missed the town weren't all that far away. It was an easy drive for cattle.

To Luke, the place looked peaceful enough, but he was wary as he rode down the dusty street. Somewhere within the town's boundaries he had enemies, enemies without names or faces. He'd made a request to the U.S. Marshals Service to be released from this assignment, for it took him too far away from Denver and his young son, Gareth. Marshal Eastburn had denied his request.

"You're the best deputy I've got," the marshal told him

1

in his blunt way, "and to clean up that mess down there, I need the best."

The stubble on Luke's face was itchy, and he wished for a shave. His clothes were covered in trail dust. He needed to find a place to clean up and get a good night's sleep, but first he intended to corral a meal. He'd been pushing hard to get here, and it had been a long time since he'd eaten. As a precaution his badge was tucked away where it couldn't be seen. The way things were, he didn't want to advertise his job until he got the lay of the land.

Coming up on his right was a small hotel and a saloon with a gaudily painted façade. It was a burgundy color trimmed in gold, a combination meant to attract the eye. Beyond the saloon was a mercantile that was almost as large as its neighbor. Snuggled between it and a gunsmith's shop was a small café. It was here that he expected to find an ally. At least that's what Eastburn had told him. He tied the blood bay to the hitching post, along with the lineback dun he'd bought before leaving Denver. A Missouri mule named Stubby, short for Stubborn, completed the trio.

His shotgun was hidden in his bedroll, but he pulled the Winchester from its scabbard and felt reassured by the weight of the Colt .44 that was strapped to his side. According to Eastburn, there was no firearms prohibition in Braxton, so no one would challenge his weapons. He was getting ready to step across the width of the boardwalk when an old codger passed in front of him, shooting Luke a strange look.

"Afternoon," said Luke politely, wondering if he knew the old man from somewhere.

Instead of replying, the fellow took off down the street as fast as his bandy legs would carry him.

Peculiar, Luke thought. He'd be willing to bet a two-and-a-half-dollar gold piece that the old man was off to report his arrival to someone.

He pushed open the café door and went inside. The room was clean and inviting. Blue gingham curtains hung at the window and matching tablecloths covered the half-dozen tables. The smell of pies baking made him even hungrier. It was early for the dinner hour, so he had the place to himself.

No sooner had he removed his hat and found a seat at a table in the corner than an attractive young woman appeared from the kitchen to take his order. He judged her to be in her early twenties, a few years younger than his own twenty-six. Her dark, glossy hair was pulled loosely into a bun. Her eyes, blue as a summer sky, betrayed a sadness that her smile tried to hide.

"You're new in town," she observed.

"Guilty as charged," he replied, "and I'm hungry as a bear that's just come out of hibernation."

"Well, I think I can take care of that. I have a nice pot of venison stew, fresh-baked apple pie, and coffee that's strong and black."

"Sounds good. I'll have some of each."

"Then I'll be only a few minutes."

Luke hadn't noticed women much since his wife's death two years earlier, but this one interested him. No doubt she was the daughter of Russ Peacock, the town council member who was supposed to be an ally.

When she returned with his food, she hesitated like she wanted to tell him something.

"Yes?" he prompted. "Is there something on your mind?"

"I was just wondering . . ." She paused and glanced out the window as if making sure there was no one directly outside.

"Are you expecting someone?" he asked.

"No," she said, turning back. "It's just that this town has eyes and ears everywhere. It pays to be cautious."

He thought of the old man he'd met on the boardwalk and had to agree.

"Is the coast clear then?"

"Yes, it appears to be. I wanted to ask if you know a man named Eastburn."

She was really asking if he was the deputy United States marshal that had been sent for.

"Yes. Fact is Jim Eastburn is my boss."

A look of relief crossed her face.

"I prefer that you keep that to yourself for now," he said. "The men I'm investigating will no doubt be suspicious of any stranger who rides into town, but at least they won't know who I am for certain."

She nodded. "I quite understand. I wouldn't want to be responsible for putting a target on your back. As you probably know, I'm Lily Peacock."

"I figured as much. I'd like to have a word with your father."

An expression of concern crossed her face.

"My father disappeared four days ago. He was riding out to the McDougal ranch, and he never arrived."

This was something Luke hadn't expected.

"Anybody go out looking for him?"

"A couple of friends and I did. But there was no sign of him."

"What about the local law?"

"If you're referring to the town marshal, he's not much. Neither is his deputy. They're no better than criminals themselves."

"That being the case, who hired them and why were they kept on?"

She looked disgusted. "The other council members," she said. "They all agreed that Morgan was a fine fellow, except for my father and the mayor, Loren Worth. He was the local gunsmith who was found murdered. He and my father usually saw eye to eye on local matters, but they were the only ones. As for the sheriff, our town is too far away for him to take much notice, in spite of Mr. Worth's murder and all the rustling that's been going on in the area."

Luke wasn't surprised. Marshal Eastburn had described the situation pretty much the same way.

"You say your father disappeared four days ago on his way to McDougal's?"

"Yes. His ranch is east of town. You see, Father and Harrison McDougal were good friends. They played chess once a week and had done so for the past few years. When Father failed to return, I rode out with Ben Coffer, the hostler over at the stable, and the boy who works for him. Mr. McDougal said he hadn't been there. He was worried too."

"I guess you reported his disappearance to the law?"

"I did. But Morgan, the town marshal, claimed it wasn't any of his business and told me that if I was smart, I'd stay in Braxton and mind the café."

"Do you think he's mixed up in this?"

She shrugged. "I wouldn't know, but then again, I wouldn't be surprised. He was hired by the council and Father refused to go along with them on many issues, including Morgan. He and Mr. Worth were opposed to many of the council's decisions. They're both gone now."

Luke had to admit that it looked suspicious. It was the outbreak of rustling and the mayor's murder that had caused Eastburn to send him to investigate. Peacock's disappearance was an unexpected addition to the trouble the area was experiencing.

"Excepting for Russ Peacock, it could be that the whole town council is corrupt," his boss had warned him. "You watch your back when you get down there. Don't trust any of them."

"Look, if I can do anything to help you," said Miss Peacock, "just let me know. There are good people in this town and you have their support."

"Thanks," he said, thinking that was nice to know, even though it wasn't apt to be much help.

"I'll leave you to your supper now," she said, and with a whirl of skirts, she was gone.

He attacked the stew like a starving man. He'd just finished the last bite of pie when the door slammed open and a fellow strutted into the café like he owned the place. He was young, maybe twenty, and skinny, with a narrow, pockmarked face. Pinned to his brick-red shirt was a shiny badge. His holster was tied down in the manner of a gunslinger.

"Lily!" he yelled. "Come on out here and bring me a cup of coffee."

His rudeness and arrogance rubbed Luke the wrong way. It pleased him that Lily was taking her time in answering his summons.

When the newcomer glanced over and saw Luke, his expression turned ugly. Luke stood and met his stare. When the fellow saw that he was well-heeled and not intimidated, his Adam's apple bobbed as he gulped. Lily appeared in the doorway that led to the kitchen.

"What do you want, Dewitt?" she demanded to know.

"I want to know who this stranger is, for one thing," he said. "Old Jubal told me there was one in town."

"That old gossip," said Lily, plainly disgusted.

"Is being a stranger a crime now, Deputy?" said Luke.

"Of course not," said Lily. "Dewitt is just trying to run my customers off."

"It's my sworn duty to see that no lowlifes come into town," Dewitt blustered.

"Well, you're too late," said Lily. "There are plenty of lowlifes already here. Now, if you want something to eat, say so."

"I ought to arrest you," said Dewitt, still glaring at Luke. "Your face is likely on a wanted dodger down at the town marshal's office."

"This man hasn't committed any crime," said Lily. "You can't arrest him. If you don't believe me, ask your boss."

Luke put the money for his meal on the table, picked up his rifle with his left hand, and prepared to leave. The deputy made his move.

"That does it, stranger. You're going to jail."

Dewitt went for his gun, but by the time his fingers touched the grips he was looking down the barrel of

Luke's .44. All the blood drained from his face and he slowly raised his hands.

"Now you are in trouble," he said, his voice quavering. "You've just assaulted an officer of the law."

"Oh, stop your babbling," said Lily. "You've made a complete fool of yourself, Benny. If this man had been an outlaw, your carcass would be bleeding all over my clean floor."

It was obvious that Dewitt didn't like being thought a fool by a beautiful woman. In fact, he didn't like the way things were going at all. He stood there, groping for a way to save face.

"I'll let you go this time," he blustered to Luke, who still had him covered. "But don't leave town before you have a talk with Marshal Morgan. He's going to have some questions to ask you."

Lily made an unladylike snorting sound that Dewitt couldn't miss. He pulled his gaze from Luke's gun barrel, turned, and beat a hasty retreat.

"Obnoxious twit," said Lily, looking after him.

Luke shoved the revolver back into his holster.

"Do be careful," she said. "Once Benny Dewitt and Boots Morgan get their hands on you, they won't let you go, and they'd both take pleasure in roughing you up. They're shameless bullies."

"What was the town council thinking when they hired a man who'd have a deputy like that?" he wondered aloud.

"Strange, isn't it? My father voted against him. But the others were all in favor. Of course, the mayor was against it, but he and Father were outvoted. After Morgan was hired, Father got in touch with some friends he thought might know something about Boots Morgan. It turns out he has a shady past. His name has been linked with cattle rustlers."

"I take it he told the council."

"Of course. Father presented his findings to the other council members right away, but they made light of it. Mike Gilmore, who owns the saloon, told him that even if the story was true, Morgan deserved a second chance. The rest of the council backed him up. They regarded my father as a troublemaker."

In Luke's line of work, he'd come across far weaker motives for killing a man.

"Would it be inappropriate to ask your name?" she said.

"Sorry, I should have introduced myself. The name's Cochran. Luke Cochran."

"Well, Mr. Cochran, you've stepped into a viper's nest."

The warning wasn't necessary. He'd been thoroughly briefed.

"You might want to talk to the council members," she said. "There's Mike Gilmore, who runs the Lucky Horseshoe saloon; Hobart Lange, the banker; Hiram Bledsoe from the mercantile; and Seth Hatch, the undertaker."

That made four council members, excluding the troublesome Peacock. He asked who the new mayor was.

"Mr. Worth hasn't been replaced. They're waiting for an election, and I understand that Mr. Lange is going to run unopposed."

Pleasant as Lily Peacock was to look at, Luke decided

she'd told him all she knew about the council and her father's disappearance. He figured it was time to ride out and have a talk with the two biggest ranchers in the district, Lyman Berry and Harrison McDougal.

"I'm going to have to leave town for a while," he said. "But don't worry. I'll be back."

She was clearly concerned. "Please be careful, Marshal. If the killers find out you're asking questions, you may disappear just the way my father did."

"I'll watch my back," he promised.

He put his hat on when he reached the door. Before stepping outside, he took the precaution of looking both ways. At the hitching post he mounted the bay, and with the dun and the mule in tow, he headed for the livery stable that was across the street and down a ways. When he got there, he found a wiry man with graying hair in charge. He guessed the man was Ben Coffer, who'd helped Lily look for her father.

"What can I do for you, mister?" he said, setting his pitchfork aside.

"I need my animals watered and fed, and I'd like a little information, if you can provide it."

"Well, I can take care of the horses and that mule of yours, but I can't guarantee the information."

The hostler had an honest look about him. What's more, he was Councilman Peacock's friend. Luke decided to put his cards on the table.

"I'm here to investigate some things that have been going on in and around your town. Do you have any ideas about what happened to Russ Peacock?"

He frowned. "No, and I sure wish I did. His girl is

worried half to death. Russ just rode out one day and never came back."

Luke dropped the subject and brought up the slain gunsmith who had been Braxton's mayor.

Coffer gave him a peculiar look when he mentioned Worth's name.

"Are you some kind of law?" he asked.

"Let's just say I'm a curious fellow with a special interest in some of the things that have been going on around here of late."

"Well, there's been a lot of rustling. That started first, and some ranchers have lost their places to the bank because of it. Then Loren Worth was shot to death outside of town. Now Russ Peacock has disappeared. He was riding out to see his friend McDougal and never got there. Me and that girl of his, and the kid who works for me, tried to track him, but we couldn't find no sign of him. I wouldn't bet a bale of straw that he's still alive."

Luke leaned against a support post as he listened to Coffer's views. The hostler seemed a decent sort.

"If'n you're the law, you might talk to Lyman Berry. He owns a big ranch west of here. Maybe he can tell you something. Berry's madder than a rooster in a rainstorm about all the cows he's lost to thieves. I even heard tell that he's ordered his men to shoot on sight anybody caught messing with his herd."

"Then I think I'll ride out and pay Mr. Berry a visit. By the way, I had a run-in with the deputy town marshal. He doesn't like me much."

Coffer spat a wad of tobacco juice into a nearby tomato can.

"That Benny Dewitt ain't got smarts enough to put his boots on by hisself. On top of that, he's got a mean streak. Guess that's why Morgan hired him. Morgan ain't no choir boy hisself, so you be careful."

When the animals had been fed and rubbed down, Luke prepared to leave. The last rays of light had faded and the lamps and lanterns around town had been lit.

"I don't mean to tell you your business," said the livery man, "but if'n I was you, I'd leave by the back way. Morgan's not in town and Dewitt is probably over at the saloon. Still, I can't be sure Dewitt will stay there, and there's no guarantee that Morgan won't ride into town any minute."

"Obliged for the warning," he said.

"Look, my name's Ben Coffer. Like most folks, I don't cotton to what's been going on around here. If you're some kind of law, then you're sure welcome. You need any help, let me know."

Luke shook his hand. "It's nice to know I've got a friend in town."

"More'n one, I'd wager."

Luke mounted up and rode out of town by way of the alley. It was deserted. When he was clear of Braxton, he headed west. Overhead, an opal moon served as a nightlight in the darkened sky. A cool wind blew down from the mountains, making a soft rustling noise in the buffalo grass.

Luke didn't want to ride onto Berry's range at night and maybe get shot for a rustler, so he veered off and headed for the nearby mountain slope. Once he was among the pines, he stopped and made camp.

After picketing the horses and mule on a patch of

grass, he cleared a circle and built a small fire. He was still full from the stew and apple pie, but coffee cut the dryness in his throat and warmed him against the mountain cold. After he'd drained the cup, he bedded down in the shadows, a little distance away from the flames. He'd kept watch on his back trail to make sure that he hadn't been followed. As far as he could tell, he'd slipped out of town unseen.

Weary from his long day's ride, Luke closed his eyes and started to drift off to sleep. He was brought fully awake by a distant howl. Wolves. There were wolves on the mountain. When the howl was answered in kind, he got up and threw more sticks of wood on the fire. Then he went back to his blankets, leaving the horses to warn him if man or animal approached.

He woke to find the darkness around him was easing into gray. During the night the fire had burned itself out, leaving only a pile of ashes. He shivered in the cold. After rekindling the fire, he put the coffeepot on to boil. Then he fixed himself a breakfast of bacon and hardtack. The food and drink warmed him considerably. By the time the sun cleared the eastern horizon, he was ready to ride.

The north side of the Berry ranch butted up against the foothills of the mountains. Back in Denver, Marshal Eastburn had showed him the layout on a map. He found a spot where he could remain hidden by pine branches while looking down on the ranch house and the surrounding area for miles. It was possible that rustlers had done the same thing before sneaking down and cutting steers from Berry's herd.

As he started to leave his vantage point, he paused.

Two riders were coming from the east. He dug out his spyglass to have a better look. He recognized one of the riders. It was Benny Dewitt. No doubt the other was Boots Morgan. He guessed he'd been wrong. Someone must have seen him leave town, heading west. They'd reported it to the deputy, who'd assumed he was heading for Berry's place. That old man from the boardwalk, maybe. He had no doubt the two lawmen from Braxton were looking for him. He figured he must have Morgan worried.

While he watched, three men emerged from the ranch house. They stood there waiting as the riders approached. They were all three armed, and they were making no secret of it. From the looks of it, the two Braxton law officers weren't all that welcome.

When Morgan and Dewitt reined up in front of the rancher and his men, Luke wished he was standing close enough to hear what was being said. Morgan looked like he was on a rant. After a couple of minutes, Berry, or maybe it was one of his men, tipped a rifle so the barrel was pointed at Morgan's middle. Morgan's hands went in the air and his lips stopped moving. Dewitt started backing his horse away. Now it was the other side's turn to rant, and he figured the talker was Berry. When he was finished, Morgan wheeled his horse and headed back the way he'd come. Dewitt was close on his heels. The man with the rifle fired two quick shots into the air. At the unexpected sound, Morgan and Dewitt took off like the devil was after them. Luke chuckled. He figured it served them right.

He continued to watch as the rancher and his men went

back inside. Then he put the spyglass away and headed downslope. No doubt Berry was wondering about the stranger who was worrying Morgan, and why Morgan was so anxious to get his hands on him.

Chapter Two

Lyman Berry and his foreman, Homer Fahl, sat at the pinewood table across from Hamilton Isham, known as Ham. Ham wasn't only a hired hand, but a longtime friend of Berry's. He was short, stocky, and a good five years younger than Berry's forty. Fahl was lean and seasoned, and he had at least a few winters on his boss. They'd all known one another for a long time. Among them, a trust had grown over the years, a trust that had been earned.

"Boss, what do you think that no-account weasel is up to?" said Isham, getting up to pour coffee for himself and the other two.

"Ham, you've known Morgan as long as I have," said Berry. "He's never up to any good. He wouldn't be wearing a badge at all if it wasn't for that addlebrained town council. Worth and Peacock were the only ones with sense. Now they're both gone."

"I wonder what happened to Peacock?" said Fahl. "He wouldn't have run off and left that girl of his, or the café, either."

16

"I don't expect so," said Berry. "Poor Russ is probably dead. The way I see it, he was giving the council too much trouble. For that matter, Worth was too."

"You ask me," said Isham, "I think Morgan killed him."

"Could have been somebody on the council," said Fahl. "I don't much cotton to any of 'em."

Their speculation was interrupted by a sudden spate of barking.

"Wonder what's wrong with Shep," said Berry, heading for the window.

Outside, the German shepherd was announcing a visitor.

"Wish Shep had been around and done that when Morgan and his sidekick rode up," said Fahl. "For two nickels, I'd have sicced the dog onto both of 'em."

"Since somebody's coming," said Berry, "I expect we'd best go meet him."

"This is getting to be a regular crossroads," Fahl complained. "A man can't drink a cup of coffee without getting interrupted."

The three of them stepped back onto the porch and watched the solitary rider from the north. He was astride a handsome lineback dun and leading a blood bay and a pack mule.

"What in thunder . . ." said Fahl. "That fellow can't be from Braxton. He's coming from the wrong direction."

"Probably wants to rustle up a job," said Isham. "Or else he's riding the grub line."

Somehow Berry didn't think so. Even from a distance, the man looked prosperous. His three animals were worth a good deal of money. Then there was the rifle in his saddle scabbard, and he wore a sidearm.

"If we hold on a bit," he said, "I expect he'll tell us what he wants."

Isham hushed the dog as the man rode up.

"Howdy," he said, pleasantlike. "I need to speak to Mr. Berry."

"And who might you be?" asked Fahl.

"Name is Luke Cochran. I'm investigating the murder of Loren Worth and the disappearance of Russ Peacock, along with some rustling that's been going on. I was hoping that Mr. Berry might be able to answer a few questions."

"I'm Berry," said the rancher, stepping forward and extending his hand. "Don't tell me Denver has finally sent down a federal marshal."

The stranger nodded. "Deputy federal marshal, although I'd appreciate it if you kept that piece of information to yourselves."

Cochran climbed down from his mount, and Berry introduced Fahl and Isham. Berry liked the look of the fellow. Cochran was tall and sturdily built, with an air of confidence about him. On top of that, he looked a man right in the eye when he spoke, something Morgan, with all of his cockiness, couldn't quite manage.

"What can I do to help you, Marshal?" he inquired.

"I was watching when a couple of fellows rode in a while ago. One looked like the deputy from Braxton."

"You're right about that. The other was the town marshal, Boots Morgan. They were looking for a stranger who'd showed up in town while Morgan was away. They say they want to question him about the rustling that's been going on. He's a 'suspicious character,' according to Dewitt. That suspicious character wouldn't by any chance be you, would it, Marshal?"

"I expect so. I had a run-in with Dewitt at the café. I think he's got his eye on Miss Peacock and saw me as competition."

"Lily Peacock is a lady who wouldn't give the likes of Benny Dewitt a second glance," said Isham.

"That's the impression I got as well. The fellow has no manners when it comes to women."

"Nor anyone else," said Berry.

He invited Luke to come in and share the last of the coffee.

"You must have been watching the place from the slope," said Berry, "else we'd have spotted you."

"Yes. I didn't think it would be smart to ride in on you last night. It might give you the wrong idea about my intentions. So I camped up there and waited for daylight. I heard you weren't too friendly to rustlers and I didn't want to be taken for one."

Berry chuckled. He liked this fellow. And who knew? He might be able to put a stop to the crime that was plaguing the area. Although he didn't see how, him being only one man.

"Don't guess you've got any clues as to who's rustling your cattle?" said Cochran.

"If I did, I'd have already hung him and his pals to the nearest cottonwood. And don't give me any lecture about leaving stuff like that to the law. We've got no law around here. Leastwise, not until you rode up."

"Do you have any suspicions then?"

Fahl and Isham exchanged glances but waited for Berry to speak.

"I think someone on the town council is behind all this and he has the other members under his thumb. The ones who wouldn't go along, Mayor Worth and Russ Peacock, were murdered. At least we suspect Russ Peacock was murdered."

"I don't think this is as simple as rustling," said Isham. "I think it's a power grab. The council has taken over the town, and they're running it the way they want to. They're walking all over people, and they're making a mockery of the law. They're probably all in cahoots."

"We have our suspicions, as you can see," said Berry. "But in the scheme of things, they're not worth a whole lot."

"The way I see it, Cochran, you have your work cut out," said Isham. "We'll help if we can."

"I appreciate that," said Luke. "I need people I can trust. There's something else too. Since I'm going back to Braxton to nose around some more, I need a place to leave my spare horse and that bullheaded mule."

"You've got it," said Berry. "But be warned, Morgan's going to be laying in wait for you in town. He's real nervous about you."

"That's why I'm waiting until dark before I ride in. I hear that Dewitt spends a lot of time at the Lucky Horseshoe saloon. Maybe Morgan does too."

"Morgan is a little smarter than his deputy," said Isham. "He's what you might call unpredictable."

"Wouldn't it be better if I sent a couple of my men with you?" said Berry.

"Thanks, but no. More men would be apt to attract attention and possibly trigger a confrontation. That's something I don't want at this point."

"I understand," said Berry. "Just remember, we're here if you need us."

Luke was invited to stay on for the midday meal. Then, after switching his gear to the blood bay, he headed back toward Braxton.

He took his time, making sure it was dark when he reached the outskirts of town. Once there, he made his way down the back alley to the livery stable, hoping that Coffer might still be there. He stepped down from the saddle and slid the door open just wide enough to squeeze through. The place was dark except for a ribbon of moonlight that flowed through a high opening. A low moan came from a dark corner of the barn.

"Who's there?" Luke called softly.

"Help me," said a weak voice that he recognized as Coffer's.

Luke found the hostler sprawled on the floor of the stable. He knelt beside him. By the light of a match he saw that the man had been badly beaten.

"Tell me, who did this to you, amigo?"

"It was Morgan and that no-account Dewitt," he gasped. "They wanted to know who you were and why you'd come to Braxton. They wanted me to tell them everything that I said to you. I told them I didn't know anything except that you wanted your animals cared for. Neither of 'em believed me."

Fury rose up in Luke like bitter bile. Morgan and his flunky had beaten a man to the edge of death because he'd exchanged a few words with a stranger at his place of business.

"I've got to get you a doctor," he said. "Is there one here in town?"

"Yes. Dr. Vanhelden. He has a place down the street, next door to the blacksmith's. His living quarters are in the back of his office, facing the alley."

"Lie still and don't move. You may have some broken ribs. I'll bring the doctor as soon as I can."

Luke hurried down the alley and knocked on Vanhelden's door, rousting him out of bed. Quickly, in as few words as possible, he told the young doctor what had happened.

"Morgan is a bully and a criminal," said Vanhelden. "So is Dewitt. I'd like to see them both run out of town. Give me a minute to get dressed and I'll get my bag and come with you."

Back at the livery stable, Luke touched a match to a lantern to shed light on the victim, as Vanhelden went to work, examining and treating Coffer's injuries.

"You've got a couple of broken ribs," he pronounced, and set about binding them tightly. Coffer groaned as the ribs were fastened in place.

"Thankfully, I don't think there's any internal bleeding," he went on. "Your nose is broken and so is your wrist. I'll set it next. I'm afraid you're going to have two black eyes and a lot of other bruises. I strongly urge you to take it easy for the next week or so. The boy, Jamie Dodd, can help out for a while, I'm sure. I expect his mother can use the money."

"Good idea," said Coffer. "I guess I'd best keep a gun handy. As far as I'm concerned, Morgan's crossed the line. He's on the wrong side of the law now. Maybe he always has been."

"Most of the folks in this town would agree with you," said the doctor. "It's just that they don't know what to do about it. Morgan and Dewitt keep people intimidated if not terrorized. They wouldn't be wearing those badges, though, if powerful men hadn't made it possible."

"Morgan's likely to jump somebody else when the mood strikes him again," said Coffer. "I wonder how many beatings and murders it's going to take before somebody does something about him."

Luke's own mood was dark. Coffer's only "crime" had been talking to a stranger who wanted his animals grained and rubbed down.

"I can see that I'm leaving my friend here in good hands," he said. "Now I've got to be going. There's something I have to tend to."

"Don't worry none about me," said Coffer. "Get on with the job that you came here to do."

Luke left the stable, crossed the street, and headed for the alley that ran behind the saloon. He could have found the Lucky Horseshoe blindfolded, from the raucous laughter and loud piano music. He wanted to look the place over before he went inside to have a face-to-face meeting with the owner.

When he neared the back door, he saw that a lighted window overlooked the alleyway. From where he stood, he had a clear view of an office. No doubt the man sitting behind the desk was Mike Gilmore, the owner of the Lucky Horseshoe, a man suspected of being involved in cattle rustling and murder. Luke's fingers brushed the grips of his pistol, and he stepped back into the shadows to wait and watch.

Chapter Three

More than anywhere else, Mike Gilmore felt at home in his office at the back of the Lucky Horseshoe. Its posh furnishings served to remind him of New Orleans, where he'd grown to manhood. He'd always admired the manners and dress of the upper class of that city, and he often pretended that he'd come from that enviable background. An accent that dripped magnolias and Spanish moss strengthened the illusion. At thirty-four, his hair was still thick and brown, with no hint of graying or loss. He worked diligently at keeping a strong, youthful physique, for he hated the sight of a flabby belly. He also indulged his taste for expensive, stylish clothes, which he ordered from his tailor in Louisiana. He was thinking of ordering a couple of new suits when a knock at the door interrupted him.

"Enter," he called.

Boots Morgan pushed the door open and walked in. The insufferable man had a smug, self-satisfied look on his face, causing Gilmore to wonder what he'd been up to now. When he finished telling his story, Gilmore stared at him in disbelief.

"You did what?" he demanded.

"Like I said, I beat the daylights out of Coffer. I was trying to find out if he knew anything about that hombre who was talking to him and Lily Peacock. The fellow who's been snooping around. Dewitt had some fun with Coffer too."

"Did you really think the stableman knew anything?" said Gilmore, deliberately not inviting Morgan to sit in one of his two upholstered visitor's chairs.

Morgan shrugged. "I thought it was worth a try."

"Well, did you find out anything?"

"I found it was easy to crack a few ribs and break a nose."

Gilmore suppressed a strong urge to wipe the smug look off Morgan's homely face.

"Boss, I figured you'd be pleased that I used what you call 'initiative.' "

Gilmore glared at him. "Look, Morgan, don't try thinking on your own. You're not any good at it. And by the way, don't call me 'boss.' "

The former cow thief looked as if he'd been backhanded. "Sure, whatever you say, Mr. Gilmore."

"I hope you didn't kill the man."

"Nah. Leastwise, I don't think I killed him. He's just a little broken and bruised is all. I left him laying there in the barn."

Gilmore sighed and wondered why Lange had insisted on hiring such an idiot and making him think he was their equal.

"Then I suppose someone will find him in the morning.

Everyone in town is going to hear what you did before the sun sets tomorrow, but none of this is to touch me. Do you understand? I'm a respectable businessman and a member of the town council. This was your doing, and you're going to have to take the consequences, whatever they may be."

Morgan looked surprised. "What consequences? I'm the law here, and I can do whatever I please."

Gilmore thought of his sleeve gun and was sorely tempted to use it. He held back only because of the trouble a shooting would cause.

"You might want to rethink that, Morgan. If you get this town riled enough, the good citizens are apt to find a rope and a nearby tree limb and rid themselves of your so-called law."

"Yeah? Well, if I hang, you're going to be hanging right there beside me, for I'll tell them everything I know."

Gilmore had no doubt that he would. Boots Morgan had become cavalier about following orders the minute he realized he had some leverage. No question about it, the man was dangerous—to the operation and to everyone involved. Something was going to have to be done about him. And about Dewitt too.

"Look, Morgan, be smart," he said. "Lay off the rough stuff. If you spot that stranger, simply watch him. See what he's up to. Then report back to me."

Morgan smirked. "Well, Mr. Gilmore, I'd sure like to do that. Trouble is Dewitt let him get away before I even got a chance to see him."

Gilmore leaned back in his leather-covered chair, forming a steeple with his hands.

"When you know something, come and tell me. Otherwise, don't draw attention to yourself—or to me. Keep your eyes and ears open. We don't know for sure that this stranger is up to anything. Not yet, anyway."

"But if he is?"

"If he is, I'll take care of it. Now, I believe you have other plans for the evening, so I won't keep you."

Having been dismissed, Morgan turned and stalked out, leaving behind an odor of horse manure from his boots and human sweat from his unwashed body.

Gilmore opened a window to let in some fresh air. He paused when he saw something move in the alleyway. For an instant, he thought it was the shadow of a man. Then, in the blink of an eye, it was gone. Probably an animal, he decided.

Back at his desk, he removed a cigar from a humidor, clipped the end, and lit it. The scent of fine tobacco removed the last trace of the odiferous toady who'd tainted what might have been a fine evening.

Luke watched the meeting through the window. It looked like the saloon owner was reprimanding the town marshal for the beating he'd given Coffer. This made sense. Gilmore wouldn't have ordered the beating; he wouldn't want to anger the townspeople. Morgan, on the other hand, was the type who enjoyed such things. When he saw Morgan leave, Luke quickly backed away, ducking out of sight when Gilmore came to the window.

Luke made his way back to the livery stable. He didn't want to leave Coffer alone. The hostler was asleep on a pallet close to where he'd fallen, the doctor still with him. As soon as Luke arrived, Vanhelden took his leave, promising to send someone by in the morning to stay with the patient.

Luke climbed into the loft and bedded down for a few hours of sleep. The next morning, before daylight, Jamie Dodd arrived, armed with an ax handle. He was a big kid for his age and looked to be able to take care of himself.

"I'm sure sorry about what happened to Mr. Coffer," he said. "The doctor came by last night and told me. If that no-account Morgan comes back, I'll let out a war whoop and give him a good whack with this here club."

Luke liked the Dodd kid. He had spunk.

"Just be careful," he warned. "Remember, there's two of them."

Most of the town was still sleeping when Luke rode out in the gray light before dawn. There was no sign of Morgan or Dewitt. The café was dark, but he figured Lily would soon be up tending to her chores. He nudged the bay in the sides, anxious to put Braxton behind him.

On the lonely ride toward the sunrise his thoughts turned to his young son, Gareth, who was in the care of his sister-in-law up in Denver. He missed the boy who looked so much like his mother and whose eyes lit up whenever Luke entered the house. It was one of the reasons he had asked to be relieved of this assignment that was taking him so far away. *Maybe I should turn in my badge and get another job,* he thought. *I can surely find something that pays a decent wage and that will let me stay closer to home.* But then, he'd been telling himself that for a long time, and nothing ever came of it.

"You're good at what you do, Cochran," Marshal Eastburn had said. "There's nobody better."

Luke doubted that. He was merely being flattered so he'd stay on and tackle the tough assignments. *One day, just wait. One day you're going to quit and settle down and watch your son grow up.*

The morning was slipping away when he spotted McDougal's ranch. The house was large and flanked by cottonwoods. He'd been expecting something smaller and simpler, more like the cabin on Berry's place.

"Come on," he said to the bay. "We won't get anything done just standing here gawking."

When he got close, a voice called out, "Hold it right there, mister. I don't know you from Adam's other ox."

Luke reined up as an old man stepped around the corner of the house, shotgun in hand.

"You Mr. McDougal?" he asked.

"Who wants to know?"

"Deputy United States Marshal Luke Cochran is doing the asking," he replied.

"It's all right, Charlie," said a second old man who suddenly appeared from the other side of the house. "This here is the feller I sent for."

"You must be McDougal then," Luke said, thinking the old men looked enough alike to be brothers.

"That I be. Now, come on in and set while you tell me what it is you're aiming to do to get my friend Russ Peacock back."

Luke tied the bay to a porch post and followed the men inside. For bachelors, the place was done up nice, with lots of women's fixings. He soon found out why when a dark-eyed woman of middle age appeared.

"This here is my housekeeper, Louisa Martinez," said McDougal with a slight brogue. "Best cook in all of Colorado."

The woman looked pleased at the compliment. "I

overheard that you are the marshal from Denver," she said. "Thank heaven you've arrived to put a stop to the killing."

"And the rustling," said the man called Charlie.

Louisa ushered Luke into a large, spotless kitchen and seated him at a round wooden table where the men joined him.

"I will have coffee for you in a minute," Louisa said. "You go ahead and talk just as if I wasn't here."

"She wants to listen in," said McDougal fondly. "Nosiest woman in the county."

"That's how I learn things," she said, not the least offended at being called nosy.

"What can you tell me about Peacock's disappearance," said Luke, "or anything else that's been going on?"

"That Southern dandy who runs the saloon is behind all this," said Charlie. "Never liked him from the day he set foot in Braxton."

"I think it's the banker," said McDougal. "Stingy as they come, he is. If he's trying to get you to put money in his bank, he's so sweet he attracts flies. But if you need to borrow, or are late with a payment, it's a different story. He treats you like trash. Lange foreclosed on a neighbor of mine who'd lost a lot of cattle to rustlers. He had to leave and go to California."

Luke asked about evidence, but there wasn't any linking either of the men to Worth's murder or Peacock's disappearance.

Louisa brought cups of steaming hot coffee, followed by freshly baked rolls and a jar of honey.

"Eat," she said. "Food helps one to think."

Luke thanked her and dug in. Whether honey-drenched rolls helped a man to think or not, they were more than welcome.

"I noticed that every fellow who was mentioned is, or was, on the city council," he pointed out. "What do you know about the other council members?"

"There're only two," said McDougal. "Hiram Bledsoe, who runs the general store, and Seth Hatch, the undertaker. I wouldn't bet that either of them is involved, though."

"Why is that?"

"Bledsoe jumps at his own shadow. He's not got enough nerve to steal a gold piece, let alone kill a man."

"Hatch ain't much better when it comes to nerve, if you ask me," said Charlie. "He's nothing but skin and bones with sunken cheeks and sunken eyes. He looks worse than a cadaver. The difference is he walks around a little better and says 'howdy' now and again."

Louisa stepped forward with the coffeepot to refill their cups. "I do not like him," she said. "A few months ago Señora Barley said that she noticed Señor Hatch had many bottles of laudanum sitting on a shelf in his back room. He was taking care of her sister who had passed away. Señora Barley thought it strange that the dead would need so much laudanum, or even the living for that matter."

"Hatch is a drug addict," said Charlie with contempt. "It's why he looks the way he does. A man who's on opium don't have no appetite for food."

Still, Hatch was elected to the town council. Either his addiction wasn't widely known or the townspeople hadn't cared.

"Who would want to get Worth and Peacock out of the way badly enough to kill them?" Luke asked.

"That takes us right back to the town council," said McDougal. "There're four members left in town. If I was you, I'd scratch Bledsoe and Hatch off the list. That leaves Lange and Gilmore. Take your pick."

"Are you still losing cattle?"

"*Nae.* Not since I wired Eastburn. But before that, I lost plenty. I couldn't catch the bloody rustlers, though. They were canny, they were. I'm a wee shorthanded, which didn't help."

Luke finished his coffee and thanked Louisa for the rolls.

"If you don't mind," he said, getting to his feet, "I'm going to have a look around your range before I ride back to town."

"Want I should go with you?" said Charlie. "I can show you where some of the rustling took place."

"I'd be obliged," said Luke. "It might save me some time."

"If you learn anything," said McDougal, "I'd appreciate knowing."

"If I learn anything, you can count on it."

Luke and Charlie rode south. The sun was high in the sky, and at their backs, clouds were forming around the mountain peaks.

"Are you and McDougal related?" Luke asked.

"Aye, as he would say. We're cousins. Harry grew up in Scotland, though. I grew up in Kentucky."

"I noticed you favor each other in looks."

"More'n that. We're both stubborn old goats. If'n you don't believe me, ask Louisa. She tells us that all the time."

Luke didn't doubt it.

After a time, he saw what looked like a line shack up ahead.

"Anybody been staying there lately?" he asked.

"Shouldn't have been. The boys have been camping out on the east range when they're not back at the bunkhouse."

"I think I'll have a look around the place."

When they rode up, Luke dismounted and looked for tracks. Wind and rain had removed any sign of who might have been there. Inside, the place looked like a hurricane had hit it.

"It ain't supposed to be this way," said Charlie, disgusted at the sight. "The boys have been instructed to keep things nice and neat."

"I doubt if this mess was made by them."

"You think them rustlers holed up here for a time?"

"Looks like maybe that's what happened."

"Harry's going to have a fit when I tell him about this mess."

Tin plates were strewn across the floor. In one corner lay a banged-up coffeepot. The scant remains of a meal sat hardening in a pan. Luke noticed something shiny on the dirt floor at the edge of a bunk. He stooped and picked up a spent cartridge. After looking it over, he slipped it into his pocket. Another quick glance around the room turned up nothing further of interest.

"Guess I'd better head back to town," Luke said. "I've seen enough."

"Then I wish you good hunting," said Charlie. "I liked Russ Peacock. He was a good friend to Harry, playing chess with him and all. And it sure looks like Russ has gotten himself into a pot full of trouble."

Luke hoped not, but Charlie was apt to be right. If Peacock was alive, he'd surely have shown up by now.

The two parted company in front of the shack. Charlie rode back toward the ranch while Luke cut across country to Braxton.

He took his time, even stopping to build a fire. Once he had it going, he put the coffeepot on to boil and made a pan of fry bread. While he was eating, he gave the town council a lot of thought. It was clear that something was going on. Cattlemen were being robbed blind. Then Lange was foreclosing on their ranches. But what were the rustlers doing with the stolen cattle? They weren't all being shipped out at one time by rail. The authorities were keeping a close watch. Besides, the brands had to be changed, and it took time for the new ones to heal. He thought it likely that the cattle were being held somewhere in the area and were shipped out later in small bunches when new brands were in place. This was something that he intended to look into.

He rode into Braxton under cover of darkness. His first stop was the livery stable. To his surprise, Coffer was sitting up, mending a harness by lantern light, a gun by his side. He looked battered and bandaged.

When he heard Luke enter, he glanced up.

"Are you going to tell me I'm supposed to be lying down, taking it easy?"

"Nope. I figure you're old enough to know what you want to do without my butting in."

"I wish everybody had your way of thinking," he said. "The doc, Miss Lily, and Jamie are all pecking at me to act sick. But I can't stand doing that. It's just not my way."

Luke began stripping the gear from his horse.

"Old habits are hard to change."

"Yes, but truth to tell, Jamie is doing all the heavy chores. I'm just supervising and making sure that none of them skunks do him like they did me."

"Strange, I don't see him anywhere around."

"He had to skedaddle. His ma sent word that she had supper ready. I can't keep the boy here all the time." Coffer patted the revolver that lay beside him. "This'll keep me company while the boy's gone."

"Just don't let 'em sneak up and get the drop on you."

Coffer indicated a three-legged stool. "Pull up a seat. I figure you've been doing some snooping around. Investigating, I mean. Did you find out anything?"

Luke sat where he could see both entries to the stable.

"Not much. McDougal and a fellow named Charlie think that Gilmore and Lange are behind all the crime that's been going on."

"Charlie's a good old boy," said Coffer. "He's McDougal's cousin, you know. From a distance, they look like two peas in a pod. McDougal talks more like he's from the Old Country, though. Charlie's way is different. More like some of the rest of us."

"I noticed."

"Did you get a chance to sample Louisa's cooking?"

"I ate some fresh-baked rolls spread with honey."

"That woman is the best cook in these parts, except maybe for the Peacocks."

Luke wasn't about to disagree.

"Charlie took me to one of their line shacks south of the house," he said. "Some owlhoots had stayed there, uninvited, and tore the place up. I figure it's where the rustlers holed up while they waited for a chance to spirit those cattle away to wherever it is that they hide them."

"Find anything that would tell you who it was?"

"Afraid not," he admitted.

"Well, I've got some news. You might be interested to know that Morgan is mad as a hornet whose nest has been smoked. Lily brought me a bowl of stew a little earlier and she was telling me about it."

"Did she say why?"

"She thinks that whoever is pulling his strings gave him what for about the beating he gave me."

The scene in the back room of the Lucky Horseshoe sprang to Luke's mind. Gilmore sure hadn't acted pleased with Morgan last evening. That was plain enough, even though he couldn't hear what was being said.

"I guess if I was in charge of whatever's going on, I'd feel the same way," said Luke, "but I'd also be worried about Morgan spilling the beans. Somehow, he doesn't strike me as the loyal type."

"I expect you're right. Anyway, he went stomping around town, giving orders and asking questions regarding your whereabouts. Said you've got Dewitt scared out of his britches with your fast draw, but he's not worried. Most likely that's because he's not about to give you a fair chance."

Luke found a rag to rub down the bay. "A man's better off if he doesn't expect a fair chance."

"Maybe. But what do you intend to do? You can't avoid him forever."

"First off, I'm going to get a good night's sleep, if you'll put me up. In the morning I'm pinning on this Deputy U.S. Marshal's badge where it can be seen a block away.

Then I'm going to pay a call on the town council members. I want to get to know each and every one of them. And while I'm at it, I want to worry them a little."

"Sounds like a fine idea to me. Just don't get yourself killed, Marshal. We've already lost two good men."

Luke didn't intend to get his name added to the list. His son needed him.

Chapter Four

Luke went to the bathhouse the next morning, where he bathed, shaved, and put on clean clothes. He was going to pay some calls.

Hiram Bledsoe turned out to be a fussy man. Luke noticed it after a customer had pawed through a stack of shirts and left them untidy. Bledsoe hurried over and quickly put them back in order. It looked like everything in his store was in its proper place. When the storekeeper wasn't at the counter toting up costs and wrapping purchases, he was wielding a feather duster against the intruding road dirt that constantly drifted in. He was clean-shaven and tidy in dress as well, at least as much as Luke could see around the large denim apron that he wore. He judged Bledsoe to be a few years the other side of forty and gathered from the man's conversations with his customers that there was no Mrs. Bledsoe waiting for him at home.

After watching and listening for a good half hour while he made his way through the store as if shopping,

Luke felt that he was being observed. It was clear that his presence was unsettling to the storekeeper. Having learned all he could, Luke selected a couple of shirts and headed for the counter.

"Did you find everything you needed?" Bledsoe inquired, eyeing Luke's shiny badge.

"I expect you'd better add a couple of boxes of .44 cartridges."

The storekeeper pulled the boxes from a nearby shelf behind the counter. Then he toted up the cost.

"I understand you were a friend of Russ Peacock," said Luke while paying for his purchases.

At the mention of Peacock's name, the storekeeper's hands started trembling, and he quickly hid them under his apron. "Yes," he said. "Russell was a fine man. I can't imagine what happened to him."

Somehow Luke didn't believe him. "When did you last see him?"

The storekeeper looked thoughtful. "That would have been the morning he left to visit his friend McDougal. He stopped by to purchase a sack of peppermints. McDougal suffers from stomach trouble, and Russell would always take him a sack of peppermints, for they soothed him."

A heavyset woman came up behind Luke with an armload of yard goods. He gave her a nod and stepped away from the counter so she could pay for her purchases. Her departure left the store empty, except for himself and the storekeeper.

"Is there something else I can do for you, Marshal?" said Bledsoe.

"I was just wondering if you knew of anyone who had a reason to kill Councilman Peacock."

He paled at the question and appeared unnerved. "No. No, Marshal, I'm afraid I don't. Russ was a good man. He had no enemies."

"I'm surprised to hear you say that," said Luke. "I heard he was at odds with the other members of the town council, including yourself."

Bledsoe's glance darted to the window as if looking for rescue. No help was in sight. "We didn't always see eye to eye, if that's what you mean," he admitted. "But in spite of that, we were all friends."

"Even Gilmore?"

He hesitated. "Yes, of course," he said unconvincingly.

Luke decided not to challenge him.

"I'll be going now," he said, "but I'll drop back later in case you remember anything that might shed light on the murders and the rustling that's been going on."

"Suit yourself, Marshal," he said, "but I've told you all I know."

As Luke reached for the door handle, he could hear the fellow's sigh of relief. If a chain is only as strong as its weakest link, he guessed that Hiram Bledsoe was the weakest link on the town council.

After packing his purchases in one of his saddle-bags, he mounted up and headed for the bank down the street. He wondered what manner of man Hobart Lange would be.

When the teller spotted his badge, he immediately ushered Luke into Lange's office. The banker was a prideful-looking fellow who appeared younger than Bledsoe. He was tall and well turned out. His sideburns were prematurely streaked with gray, and a pair of pince-nez glasses was clipped to his nose. He stepped forward to shake hands.

"Well, well, we meet at last," he said. "I've been hearing about the stranger who's come to town, but I had no idea until a few minutes ago that you were a United States marshal. Have a seat, if you will."

"Actually, I'm a deputy U.S. marshal," Luke amended, "but most folks just refer to me as a marshal. It's easier to say, and I'm actually here on behalf of the federal marshal."

"Who sent for you?" he queried as he took his seat behind the desk and motioned Luke to a visitor's chair.

It occurred to Luke that a man in Lange's position would want that information real bad. That is, if he was in on the rustling and killing.

"United States Marshal James Quinton Eastburn, who's stationed in Denver," he replied, choosing to misunderstand the banker's question.

Lange cleared his throat.

"What I meant was, who around here sent for a deputy marshal, and why?"

"I'd think the 'why' was pretty obvious. There's been a murder, probably two, and that's not to mention all the rustling that's been going on. Don't you think that's enough reason?"

Lange fixed him with a stare. "Oh come, my good fellow, aren't you exaggerating?"

The man was like an actor who was overplaying his role.

"Exaggerating?" Luke said. "Now why would I do that?"

"So there's been one shooting, and another fellow has taken off for parts unknown. A few head of cattle have been rustled here and there. That sort of thing happens in a land where law enforcement is spread a bit thin. Anyway, our troubles are a job for the county sheriff, or maybe even Morgan. But it's certainly not anything that should come to the attention of the United States Marshals' office." Behind the pince-nez glasses, his beady eyes watched Luke's face closely.

"I assure you that Marshal Eastburn feels differently. Sheriff Leavy has all he can handle elsewhere, and neither Morgan nor Dewitt could find their own backsides with a map and a lantern. I'm surprised that you and the other council members would agree to hire such men, let alone tolerate them."

Lange's expression hardened. "Look here, Cochran, we don't need some outsider from Denver telling us how to run our business here in Braxton. If that's all you're here for, you'll have to excuse me. I have business to take care of."

With that the banker got up and opened the office door. "Good day, Deputy Marshal," he said coldly.

Gone was the façade of a kindly businessman. In its place was arrogance and rudeness.

Luke got up and left the bank without a word. The sunshine outside was a relief after the stuffy office that smelled of stale cigar smoke. Lange had made himself look guilty as sin.

Luke decided that it was time to send a wire to Denver. He wanted some background information on Morgan and Dewitt. While he was at it, he'd have Eastburn see what he could dig up on Lange, Gilmore, Bledsoe, and Hatch as well. To maintain secrecy, it would be unwise to send the wire from Braxton. Instead, he would have to ride over to Parsons and send the wire from there. First, though, he decided to make a stop at the café for breakfast. He wanted to tell Lily what he'd found out. Her expression brightened when she saw him walk in.

"I've been afraid for you," she said.

The morning hour was late, so the café was empty. They could speak openly without fear of being overheard.

She served him a small steak and three eggs that had come from her own flock of hens. Then she brought the coffeepot and filled a cup for him and one for herself.

Sitting across from him, she waited for news. He couldn't help but notice how fresh and pretty she looked in spite of a few worry lines.

"Sorry, I can't bring you word of your father," he said.

"Then at least there's still hope that he's alive."

He didn't have to tell her what she already knew. The odds were overwhelming that her father was dead.

"I'm going to ride over to Parsons and send a wire to my boss. See what I can find out about certain people's backgrounds. I don't trust the telegrapher here to keep his mouth shut."

"And you shouldn't," she agreed. "Henry Moss is an old gossip, even worse than Jubal Bench."

"I want to leave without Morgan or anyone seeing me," he said. "I don't want to be followed, and they're out looking for me."

"Then they'll be watching anyone who leaves town. What you need is a diversion."

Before she could elaborate, the door swung open and Dewitt came swaggering in.

He stood scowling at them.

"What is it you want, Benny?" Lily asked, using a name that he obviously didn't like.

"I'm here to inform Cochran that Marshal Morgan wants to see him at the jail. Right now! I've been sent to escort him—bound and gagged and at gunpoint if need be."

Word traveled fast. Everyone in Braxton must know his name by now, as well as the fact that he wore a badge.

"Hey, I'm talking to you," said Dewitt, for Luke was pointedly ignoring him.

"You're not saying anything of interest to me," said Luke, "and I've got nothing to say to the town clown."

Dewitt's face flushed in anger. His bully tactics weren't working, and he must be remembering the humiliation he'd suffered the last time he'd tried to outdraw Luke.

"Go away, Benny," said Lily. "Stop pestering us."

Dewitt swore under his breath. "You can bet that Marshal Morgan's going to make you sorry you was ever born," he blustered before storming out of the café.

"You said something about a diversion, before we were so rudely interrupted," Luke reminded Lily.

"There's a ramshackle shed out back that Father was meaning to tear down. There's no wind to speak of today, so I think it would be safe to start a fire. With all eyes focused on that, you can ride out of town without anyone being the wiser."

It sounded like it might work.

"Give me twenty minutes to get ready before you start anything," he said. "And be careful you don't get caught."

When he got back to the livery stable, he found that Coffer wasn't alone. Ham Isham had ridden in, bringing the dun along with him.

"Thought you might have need of a fresh horse by now," said the Berry hand.

"While he was waiting, I've been filling him in on what's been going on," said Coffer.

"Thanks for bringing the dun," said Luke. "I've got to get to Parsons right away. Lily Peacock is creating a diversion so I can get out of town without Morgan and his partner on my heels."

"Him and Dewitt are nothing but outlaws," said Isham. "Why don't you let me ride along with you, Cochran? Might be you could use some help."

"Sure," Luke agreed. "I'd be glad for your company. I need to send a wire to my boss. See if he can find out what some of these characters were doing before they moved into town."

Quickly he switched his gear from the blood bay to the dun. No sooner had he finished than there were shouts from the street.

"Fire! Fire! Get the bucket brigade!"

"That's Lily's diversion," he said. "Let's get going."

They managed to get out of town without attracting any notice. Then they quickly put distance between themselves and Braxton.

Parsons lay to the east about twenty miles. It was the larger of the two towns, and Luke was acquainted with the local lawman. He and Pete Brosseau had fought side by side down at Glorietta Pass when the Texans tried to take over New Mexico and Colorado for the Confederacy. Pete was honest, and he was a right fair town marshal to boot, from what he'd heard.

"Do you suppose any of them coyotes back in Braxton are wanted by the law?" Isham wondered aloud.

"I wouldn't be surprised. Anyway, we'll soon know for sure."

Because of their late start, they had to camp west of Parsons for the night. Luke built a small fire in a depression, one that couldn't be seen from a distance. He was on the lookout for enemies from Braxton, but because this was Ute country, he was on the lookout for them as well. They might go about their own business, but as one old-timer put it, Utes are "notional."

While they ate their makeshift meal, Isham became talkative.

"The boss is plenty worried. He's lost a lot of cattle and can't afford to lose any more."

"Have you worked for Berry long?"

"You might say that. Frankly, I've lost track of the years. Knew him before we came to Colorado. He's as fine a man as they make 'em."

Luke had come across a lot of good people in Braxton and the surrounding area, besides Lyman Berry. They didn't deserve to be run over roughshod by criminals.

Later, in the darkness, he and Isham slept. The horses were picketed nearby and would warn of anyone's approach.

At first light they were up and soon on their way to Parsons. When they entered the town, it didn't seem too unlike Braxton to Luke, only a little bigger. They went immediately to pay a visit to Pete Brosseau.

"Well, well, it's sure good to see you, Cochran," said the tall, lanky lawman when they entered his office. He got up and pumped Luke's hand. "I heard you were working up in Denver."

Luke introduced Isham.

"I still live in Denver," he said, "but my boss sent me down to Braxton on account of all the rustling that's been going on and the mayor's murder. By the time I got there, a member of the town council had mysteriously disappeared. There's a good chance that he's been killed."

Brosseau grimaced. "I've been hearing stories about the goings-on there. Sit down, both of you, and have some coffee. Fill me in on what's been happening."

Briefly, Luke outlined Braxton's troubles and added what little he'd been able to find out.

"The town council looks mighty suspicious to me," he went on. "To top it off, Morgan and Dewitt have way overstepped their bounds. They beat Coffer, the hostler, half to death because he was seen talking to me."

"It doesn't sound good," said Brosseau thoughtfully. "I'm surprised that Eastburn didn't send some help along."

"He's too shorthanded right now to spare any more deputies, and speaking of Eastburn, I'm here to send him a wire as soon as the telegraph office opens. I want to know if anyone on the council, or that so-called town marshal and his deputy, has anything in their past we should know about."

Brosseau got up and refilled their cups.

"From what you've told me," he said, "I wouldn't be surprised."

Luke and Brosseau reminisced about the days they'd spent in New Mexico while Isham listened. When it came time for the telegraph office to open, Luke and his partner finished their coffee and took their leave.

"I wish you good luck," said Brosseau. "I hope you can get Braxton cleaned up for the decent folks who live there."

Luke hoped so too. "Thanks," he said. "We're going to need all the luck we can get."

When they got to the telegraph office, Isham opted to wait outside. "I'll keep lookout in case Morgan or any of them others followed us," he said. "I don't expect they did, but you never know."

Inside, Luke found a young telegrapher on duty.

"Help you?" the man inquired.

"I need to send a wire."

He took the stub of a pencil that was offered and wrote out a message on the yellow form that was provided.

Luke was familiar with Morse code, so after paying the fee, he hung around to make sure the telegrapher got it right.

"I'll be back later for the reply," he said.

He and Isham were headed for a nearby café with the intention of cornering a stack of flapjacks, when Luke stopped in his tracks. He saw a man leave the apothecary shop who fit the Braxton undertaker's description.

"Isn't that Hatch?" he said.

"It sure as sin is," said Isham.

Hatch hurried down the street in the opposite direction.

"He sure was carrying a big package," said Isham. "I wonder what he bought."

"Well, it's my job to be nosy, and I know one way to find out. I'll go in there and ask the proprietor."

He paused first and watched Hatch mount his horse at the end of the street after stowing the package in one of his saddlebags. When the undertaker rode off in the direction of Braxton, Luke stepped inside the apothecary shop. Isham followed.

The grizzled old man behind the counter asked what they wanted.

"That fellow who was just in here, what did he buy?" said Luke.

The old man eyed his badge and gave him a suspicious look. "What my customers buy is confidential," he said. "Frankly, it's none of your business."

Luke reached across the counter and grabbed him by the shirtfront. "It does happen to be my business, and lives may depend on what I find out. If you know what's good for you, you'll talk."

The old man's eyes widened with surprise. He grabbed Luke's wrists and tried to wiggle loose. "Let me go," he squeaked. "I'll tell you what you want to know."

"That's better," said Luke as he released his hold. "Now, what did Hatch buy when he was in here?"

"It was laudanum. I have a supplier, and Dr. Hatch has a lot of people coming to him in pain, needing the relief it gives."

Luke recalled what Louisa had told him when he was at McDougal's ranch. "The man's an undertaker," he said, unable to disguise his disgust. "The people who come to Hatch are dead and beyond pain. Hatch is an addict."

The old man paled. "I didn't know," he said. "I thought the medicine was going to needy patients."

"Let's get out of here," said Isham. "I've heard enough."

"Another one of Braxton's distinguished council members," Luke muttered under his breath.

After they left the apothecary shop, they found a café and put their feet under the table for a while. When they'd finished eating breakfast, they headed back to the telegraph office to see if a reply had come in.

"There's nothing yet," said the telegrapher, "but you're welcome to wait."

While Isham went outside to build himself a smoke, Luke found a place on one of the benches that lined the walls.

Luke had done a good deal of waiting in his life, but it wasn't anything he favored. His thoughts turned to his four-year-old son, Gareth. He was grateful that the little boy had a good home with his late wife's sister, Joanna Simpson, and Joanna's husband, Clark. Still, he wanted to play a much bigger part in Gareth's life, especially now that his son was getting older. But if Eastburn kept sending him so far away on assignments, it wasn't likely to happen. *Maybe you need to change jobs,* he thought again, as he'd done so often before. *Get into a line of work with regular hours like clerking in a store.*

The telegraph began to clickety-clack, grabbing his full attention. By the time the telegrapher got the message written down, he already knew what it said.

Boots Morgan had been caught red-handed rustling cattle up north and was nearly lynched by those who captured him. A couple of his partners had gotten him away by force of arms. Then he robbed a stage and did time in the penitentiary. When he got out, he beat an old couple to death and robbed them of their life savings. His sketch was on a wanted poster.

It was no surprise that Dewitt was wanted too. He'd been arrested in Denver on three occasions for beating and robbing drunks. One of his victims died, but Dewitt managed to escape.

Eastburn hadn't found anything on the four council members yet, but he reminded him that they could be using assumed names, and they might even have altered their appearances to some degree.

At any rate, Luke had plenty of reason to arrest and jail both Morgan and Dewitt. Afterward, he'd put someone in charge until the town council got around to hiring Morgan's replacement. Trouble was, he didn't trust a soul on the council, and he figured the two outlaws were working for at least one of the members—and possibly all of them. He tucked the message into his vest pocket and went out to break the news to Isham.

"I'm not surprised," said his partner. "I doubt anybody else will be either. What are you planning on doing?"

"I'm going to arrest both of them and lock them in a cell until they can be extradited to Denver. Then, for the time being, I'm going to deputize a man and put him in charge of the local law."

"Got anybody in mind?" Isham inquired as they mounted up to head west.

"Yep. I think you'd be a good man for the job."

Isham gave a start. "You think so? I'm willing, but I don't see how you're going to pull this off. Morgan's going to put up a fight, and so is Dewitt. What's more, the council won't stand for it."

"I'll take care of Morgan and that clown of his. As for the council, they're not going to have a say. The next time I hear from Eastburn, they're apt to be warming jail cells themselves."

"You make it sound easy."

"Oh, it won't be easy. None of 'em will throw in the towel without a fight. But Eastburn thought something like this might happen when he sent me. So, just in case, he sent along a couple of badges. I've got one for you, and as soon as I swear you in, it'll all be legal. You'll be working for me and the U.S. Marshals' office. The council won't have any say about it. Their own men are wanted criminals."

Before they got to town, Luke reined up.

"All right, Isham, raise your right hand and repeat after me . . ."

A few uttered words and the deed was done. Luke tossed him a badge.

Isham pinned it on his shirt and they started off again.

"You're going to need some help," said Luke. "You got anybody in mind you can trust?"

"Homer Fahl," he said without hesitation. "He's a good man, and I'd trust him with my life."

Luke had to agree that Berry's foreman was a good choice. "Will Berry be able to do without him for a while?"

"The boss wants Braxton cleaned up. I expect he'd make any sacrifice to get the job done."

"Then I think we should bypass town and go pick up Fahl. That is, if he's willing to pin on a badge. Afterward, we'll all head for town and I'll arrest Morgan and Dewitt."

"You realize that there's going to be an outcry from the council once you make the arrests."

Luke didn't doubt it. "I reckon I'd be disappointed if there wasn't."

He wondered how it would affect the council to have the two thugs they'd hired cooling their heels in jail. He hoped it would shake them up a little and cause someone to make a mistake.

Berry saw them coming as they rode up. Right off, he noticed the badge on Isham's shirt and grinned. "Guess I've lost my best hand," he said.

"It's only temporary, Boss," said Isham. "But the way things are, I think Cochran here needs me more."

"I also need your foreman for a spell, if you can spare him," said Luke, "and if he's willing to come along with us."

"I'll spare him gladly, but you'll have to ask Fahl if he wants to play lawman."

Berry's foreman was sent for and the situation explained.

"Sure, I'll come along," Fahl agreed. "But this is only until you get them thieves and killers behind bars. I'd a lot rather deal with cows than criminals."

Luke let him know that he understood the conditions. Then he swore in his second deputy.

The sun was sinking over the mountains to the west. It was too late to start for Braxton. Luke took a few minutes to pay a visit to his mule, Stubby, who seemed to be content with his new surroundings.

Later, as he ate supper with Berry and his new deputies, they speculated on what Eastburn might find out about the council members.

After a good night's sleep, Luke, Isham, and Fahl headed out at dawn.

"Morgan is said to be pretty fast with a gun," said Fahl as they were nearing town. "On the other hand, it was Morgan who said it."

"Well, I happen to know that Dewitt is slow as molasses," said Luke. "I think he's realized that, though."

"Still, you don't have to be all that fast when you're shooting a fellow in the back," said Isham. "Morgan and Dewitt both strike me as back-shooting types."

"We'll have to watch out," said Luke. "And don't forget, Morgan and Dewitt aren't the only enemies we have. There's more than one who wouldn't mind putting a bullet between our shoulder blades."

He could think of at least four men who might try to keep him from returning to Denver and hugging his son again.

Chapter Five

When Luke rode into town flanked by two deputies wearing badges, he attracted attention. Sensing a show, the folks on the street hurried to tell others. By the time he and his deputies reined up in front of the jail, the boardwalks on both sides of the street were filling with spectators. He motioned them back.

Morgan's horse was tied to the hitching rail right next to Dewitt's, so it was likely they were inside. Luke dismounted.

"We're right behind you," said Isham. "But watch out."

Stepping onto the boardwalk, Luke saw Morgan cross in front of the window with a gun in his hand. He managed to jump out of the way an instant before a shotgun blasted a hole in the door. Spectators scattered like chickens in a rainstorm. Isham, who was hugging the dirt, brought up his pistol and fired through the hole three times as rapidly as he could squeeze off the shots.

Luke ducked around the corner of the jail and made his way to the back door.

"Hey, out there!" shouted Dewitt. "Stop shooting! I'm hurt bad!"

"Throw out your weapons!" Isham ordered. "Then both of you come out with your hands in the air."

Luke was rounding the back corner of the jail and could see the door. It eased open and Morgan stepped out.

"Hold it right there!" said Luke. "You're not going anywhere. Drop your gun!"

Morgan called him a string of names that would have scandalized the ladies of the Missionary Society. Still, having no choice, he did as he was told.

When Luke marched Morgan back inside, Isham and Fahl had their guns trained on Dewitt. There was blood on Dewitt's sleeve, and he was whimpering.

"We'll put 'em in separate cells," said Luke. "Then I'll send for the doctor."

"You're a dead man, Cochran," Morgan growled. "I've got powerful friends, and you won't be leaving this town alive."

Luke shoved him into the back cell and locked the door. Dewitt was ushered into the next one.

"Hurry up with that doctor," begged the wounded outlaw.

"I'd feel sorry for you," said Luke, "if you hadn't helped beat up a good man for no reason at all."

"It wasn't me," Dewitt lied. "It was Morgan. All I did was watch."

"Shut your mouth!" said Morgan, who was standing with both hands on the bars like he wanted to pull them apart.

Luke reached in and grabbed Morgan's badge, ripping it from his shirt.

"You won't need this anymore," he said. "Not where you're going."

Next, he confiscated Dewitt's badge. Maybe now he'd find out exactly who Morgan's friends were and how far they'd go to save his neck.

He sent one of the bystanders to fetch Dr. Vanhelden.

Coffer pushed his way through the crowd to enter the office. He still looked like he'd been used as a punching bag.

"Anybody hurt?" he inquired, staring at the mutilated door.

"Besides the remains of that door you're looking at," said Luke, "only Dewitt was wounded, and I don't think it's serious. Anyway, Vanhelden is on his way."

"He can take his time as far as I'm concerned. I heard the shotgun blast over at the stable and thought I'd see if you needed some help." He had a pistol with scarred grips tucked in his belt.

"I appreciate your support," said Luke.

"I'm getting those spectators out of here," said Fahl.

He went out and shooed the townspeople away from the jail. "Show's over," he said. "Go on about your business."

"Just how long do you think you can hold me?" Morgan called from his cell.

"As long as necessary," said Luke. "We're sending you back to Denver where you're wanted by the authorities."

"You ain't sending me nowhere. The town council is going to chew you up and spit you out, all three of you."

Luke left him to bluster to the walls of his cell and turned his attention to the shot-up door.

"It's too damaged to repair," said Isham. "The town's going to have to spring for a new one."

"I've got an idea about that," said Coffer. "I know where to get one free of charge. Been standing in the barn for a year now. It came off a store that was torn down over at Trinidad."

"Need help getting it here?" said Luke, as he followed the hostler outside.

"Nah. I'll get Jamie Dodd and one of his friends to do it. You're needed right where you are."

Luke looked over to see the banker Lange hotfooting it down the boardwalk toward the jail. He was under a full head of steam.

"What's the meaning of this, Cochran?" he demanded to know in a voice that carried over most of the town. "You can't shoot at lawmen and then lock them up like common criminals."

Luke planted his feet on the boardwalk and waited for Lange to come to a stop. "Folks around here can tell you that the so-called lawmen were shooting at us first," answered Luke. "That shattered door is proof, if proof is needed. Besides, both Morgan and Dewitt have paper on 'em. They're wanted in Denver for murder and rustling, and I'm holding them until the Denver authorities can extradite them."

"Unconscionable lies!" he said. "I won't stand for it! You go in there and unlock those cells right now."

Luke glanced around to see if he could spot any of Lange's men who might be positioned to shoot him. The audience of townspeople hadn't diminished. If anything, the crowd of onlookers had grown.

Quickly, he stepped back inside the jail.

Lange followed. "Give me the keys, Cochran. I'll let them out myself."

"Touch those keys and I'll lock you up too," said Luke. "I may do it anyway. I think you knew who Morgan was and what he'd done when you hired him. That goes for Dewitt too."

"Nobody's going to believe your silly allegations," he blustered.

"They will as soon as the wanted dodgers and the authorities from Denver arrive. Now get out of here before you find yourself sharing a cell with Morgan."

"The council is going to meet about this," he sputtered. "And I'm going to wire the territorial governor, who happens to be a friend of mine. He'll have your badge."

"Send all the wires you want," said Luke.

On his way out, Lange bumped into the doctor, who was coming in. He shoved on past without an apology.

"Looks like you've ruffled some feathers," Vanhelden observed.

"And drawn some blood. At least one of my deputies did. Dewitt's in a cell. He needs attention."

While the doctor went to have a look at the wounded prisoner, Fahl stationed himself in front of the jail. Isham went out back to keep watch. Luke stepped out in time to see Jamie Dodd, Coffer's helper, coming down the street with another kid about his age. They were toting the heavy new door.

"The boss sent this," said Dodd when they got to the jail. "It won't take me long to put it up. No charge."

"I'd be obliged," said Luke, before going back inside.

Vanhelden finished cleaning and dressing Dewitt's wound.

"He was lucky," said the doctor, closing his bag and preparing to leave. "I didn't even have to remove a bullet. It went through cleanly. I gave him a dose of laudanum to settle him down. He'll be good as new."

"I'll be over to pay you later," said Luke, "unless, of course, you want to submit a bill to the town council."

Vanhelden grimaced. "If I leave it to Lange and the rest of them, I'll never get paid. Just stop by when you get a chance."

Since his deputies had everything under control at the jail, and the new door was almost in place, Luke decided to pay a visit to Braxton's undertaker, who was conspicuously absent.

Inside, the walls of the funeral parlor were papered in a grim shade of maroon, giving the place a gloomy feel. The carpet was maroon as well. The room contained a settee and four or five chairs that were upholstered in dark brown horsehair. A tall oak grandfather's clock stood in one corner, ticking loudly as if counting down the seconds of a man's life.

Luke barely had a chance to look around before the cadaverous, sunken-eyed Hatch appeared from behind a curtained doorway.

"Well, well, Marshal Cochran, I was wondering when you'd be paying me a visit. I understand you've already been to see my good friends Hobart and Hiram."

He was referring to Lange and Bledsoe.

"I see that news gets around fast here in Braxton. I stopped by to tell you that Morgan and his deputy have been arrested. They're wanted criminals."

"Not surprising," said Hatch. "What the two of them did to Mr. Coffer is unforgivable."

"Then I guess you'll be glad to know that I've sworn in a couple of deputies, Ham Isham and Homer Fahl. They'll be serving as law officers for the town, at least temporarily."

Hatch nodded. "Not a bad choice, Marshal. Not a bad choice at all."

Luke was surprised at the councilman's attitude. "I'm afraid Banker Lange doesn't agree with you. He's fit to be tied and he's threatened to call a meeting of the council. He also told me he was going to wire his friend, the governor, and get me fired."

Hatch chuckled, a sound that was incongruous with his appearance.

"Hobart thinks he runs the council. Beyond that, he thinks he runs the town. He runs neither, although Hiram Bledsoe and Mike Gilmore are often intimidated by his bullying manner."

"And you're not?"

"Of course not. Bluster and bravado, that's all it is. Mostly, I ignore it."

"But you voted with the council to hire Morgan," Luke reminded him.

"Guilty as charged. However, in retrospect, I think we should have checked up on him first. We should have checked on Dewitt too."

"Russ Peacock didn't go along with the rest of the council. I understand that Mayor Worth was opposed too."

Luke watched Hatch's expression, which didn't change.

"They were perhaps wiser than the rest of us," he replied.

"They are also gone."

This time Hatch's facial muscles tensed, as did the rest of his body.

"It was unfortunate about Loren Worth. He was a good man, and he left a lovely wife. Still, we mustn't give up hope of finding Russ alive."

"He's been missing a long time now. Can you think of any other explanation for his disappearance?"

Hatch got the same regretful look on his face that he no doubt reserved for the surviving family members of the dearly departed.

"I'm afraid that I cannot. Is there anything else I can do for you, Marshal? I really need to excuse myself, as I have duties that need my attention."

"No, sir. I've taken up enough of your time. But I may have questions for you later on."

"Then I look forward to seeing you again, and I bid you good day."

With that, the undertaker disappeared back through the curtains. Luke was glad to leave that maroon-lined cave and feel the sunshine on his face.

It was clear that Hatch was an addict. But then, lots of respectable people were laudanum addicts. That didn't necessarily make him a killer.

Since Mike Gilmore was the only council member whom Luke hadn't personally spoken with, he decided it was time to head for the Lucky Horseshoe.

In this morning hour the saloon was quiet: no raucous

laughter, no piano music, no buzz of conversations spilling out. It was as if everyone was resting and gearing up for the evening hours. He pushed through the swinging doors and found himself in an empty room. The Lucky Horseshoe wasn't your typical down-at-the-heels establishment that so often sprang up in frontier communities. There were no rough-hewn boards laid across barrels to make a bar, no rotgut poured into chipped cups or mismatched glasses. Instead, a mahogany bar stretched halfway across the rear part of the room, backed by a gilt-framed mirror. Polished glassware sat neatly on a shelf. The tables and chairs all matched, and there was a roulette wheel at one end of the room near a staircase. A piano stood at the other. Having stolen a glimpse at the inside of Gilmore's office, Luke would have been surprised to find the place less opulent.

He heard steps on the stairs and glanced up to see a slender, attractive woman in a plain green dress descending. Her dark hair was pulled back, giving her a schoolmarm look. When she reached the bottom step, she smiled at him.

"You're a little early, aren't you, cowboy?"

He returned the smile. "Actually, I'm Deputy Marshal Cochran, and I needed to have a few words with Mr. Gilmore if he's available."

She took a quick glance at his badge and failed to hide the flicker of fear in her eyes.

"I'm afraid that Mr. Gilmore isn't up yet. He works late, you know."

"Guess I should have thought of that," said Luke. "Tell you what, I'll come back later on."

"There's no need to rush off," she said. As she approached, he caught the scent of lilacs. "Have a drink on the house. I'll get it for you."

"No thanks," he replied. "It's too early, and besides, I'm working."

"Well, it's nice to meet you, Marshal. My name is Holly. Stop in anytime if you change your mind about that drink."

Back on the street, the scent of Holly's perfume lingered. One thing you could say for Gilmore, he had good taste. Still, Gilmore was on his list of murder suspects, right up near the top with Hobart Lange. Not that he'd trust any of them, not even the pretty Holly.

He was heading back to the jail when Lily caught up with him.

"Are you all right?" she asked, her voice filled with concern.

"I'm fine. The only one who got hurt was Dewitt, and his wound wasn't serious."

A look of relief crossed her face. "Maybe I shouldn't say this, but Benny was asking for it."

"No more than Morgan. But they're both going up to Denver to stand trial."

"Almost everyone in town is relieved to be rid of those two. Ham Isham is well known and respected. Mr. Fahl is respected because he's Lyman Berry's foreman. You couldn't have made better choices to represent the law."

Lily was a fine-looking woman in spite of the worry lines around her eyes, no doubt caused by the bad time she'd been going through. If they found Russ Peacock dead, the news would give her even more pain.

"Lange was pitching a fit when he heard what I'd done," said Luke.

"Well, the power of the press is behind you."

"What press?" said Luke, wondering why he hadn't heard of Braxton's newspaper.

"Oh, it's not much to brag about. Niles Sinclair has a small office next to the feed and grain store. He's operating on a shoestring and he doesn't have a sign up yet. He puts out a paper whenever the spirit moves him or something newsworthy happens. Calls it the *Braxton Bugle*."

"How does he make a living with such a haphazard approach?"

She stepped closer and spoke in a voice that was barely above a whisper. "Don't tell anyone, but some of us women suspect that Niles writes those dime novels about the heroes of the West."

Luke wondered why there was a need for the secrecy. It didn't sound like too bad a job to him, at least not for an unsuccessful newspaperman. A fellow had the right to eat, and dime novels weren't against the law.

"I've got to get back to the café," said Lily. "I just needed to know that you were all right."

"I thank you kindly for your concern," he replied, liking the woman even more than before.

He decided to pay the editor of the *Braxton Bugle* a visit. Newspaper reporters were notoriously nosy. Sinclair might know something about the council that would shed light on the murder of the mayor and disappearance of Peacock. Sinclair might be a valuable ally. Then too, he might be in cahoots with the council.

Chapter Six

We've got to do something about that infernal marshal," said Lange as he stood over Gilmore's desk, his face ruddy with anger. "He's got Morgan and Dewitt locked up in the jail, and he's questioning everyone. My threats don't seem to faze him."

Gilmore sat silent through his tirade. When Lange paused for breath, he heard steps outside the door. He put his finger to his lips to silence the banker. An instant later, there was an insistent knock.

"Over there," he mouthed, pointing at the corner behind the door, where Lange couldn't be seen from the doorway.

"Who is it?" he called, giving Lange time to conceal himself.

"It's Holly. Someone was just here to see you."

He opened the door but didn't invite her in.

"I thought you ought to know," she said. "Marshal Cochran was in here a little while ago looking for you.

I sent him away, but he said he needs to talk to you and he's coming back later."

A feeling of dread knotted in Gilmore's stomach even though a visit from Cochran was not unexpected. Lange and Bledsoe had each received one.

"You did right, Holly," he assured the pretty young barmaid. "Keep an eye on the door, though. See that he doesn't sneak back here to my office. I don't want to have to deal with any surprises."

She gave him a smile, brightening his mood. "You know you can count on me, Mike."

"I know, sweetheart. Now, I'm sure you have things to do, so I won't keep you."

He watched her walk away before closing the door.

"I told you that marshal was going to keep on making trouble," said Lange, moving out into the room again. "One of us is going to have to take care of him."

"Don't involve me," said Gilmore. "I don't want anything to do with killing a United States marshal, deputy or otherwise."

"I didn't take you for a coward."

"Take me for one if you want, but Cochran's murder would bring the whole blasted lot of them down on this town, and down on us in particular. They wouldn't leave a shot glass or bank note unturned."

"Then we'll simply make his death look like an accident."

Gilmore couldn't have been more exasperated with his partner. "You're joking, of course. After what's happened to Worth and Peacock, I don't think Cochran's boss is going to sit up there in Denver and accept our word that his deputy's death was an accident. He'd be down here tearing this place apart."

"What if we break Morgan out of jail and pay him to kill Cochran? Then one of us can kill Morgan and make it look like he was hit in a shootout with the marshal. In fact, I don't know why we can't blame everything on Morgan."

Gilmore sat down behind his desk while Lange eased himself into a chair as well. Gilmore leaned back, closed his eyes, and thought about his situation. A scapegoat was what Lange was suggesting. The way Morgan had messed things up, he probably deserved that fate. Still, the plan was impromptu, and Cochran wasn't dumb. It was way too easy for something to go wrong.

"Your plan sounds good," he started out diplomatically. "However, a quickly hatched plan rarely works the way it's supposed to. What if it fails? What if Cochran kills Morgan?"

Lange shrugged his shoulders. "That's nothing to worry about. It would save one of us from doing it. We'd find some other way to get rid of Cochran."

"All right, but what if Cochran fails to kill Morgan? What if Morgan is only wounded and disarmed? I've no doubt the marshal could make that little bantam rooster talk. He'd tell about the rustlers you hired to bankrupt the ranchers. He'd probably blab to him about your scheme to become influential in politics when Colorado becomes a state. Not least of all, he'd tell how you lured Worth to his death and how you shot Russ Peacock."

"Stop right there!" Lange ordered, not liking to have the situation bluntly laid out. "It appears that my plan is flawed, so we'll let it go for now. But since Morgan is likely to betray us in return for a lighter sentence, we have to do something."

"I see your point," Gilmore admitted. "However, the one I'm most worried about is Bledsoe. If the marshal keeps putting pressure on him, he's apt to fold. Hatch doesn't worry me. That opium he doses himself with all the time keeps him steady. But Bledsoe is a nervous Nellie."

"Don't worry, Hiram won't talk. He's well aware that there's a rope waiting for him in Kansas if he does."

"There's a rope waiting for you too, Lange. That is, if the marshal finds out your real name."

"Well, he won't get it from Bledsoe, because Bledsoe doesn't know it. Neither does Hatch. You're the only one who does."

The look the banker gave Gilmore made a chill run down his spine. He was the only one who knew Lange's secret, and Lange wasn't a trusting man.

"Go have a drink," he said. "It's on the house, and it'll steady your nerves. I assure you, Cochran's not going to find out a thing. He'll hit a stone wall, and eventually he'll get tired of looking. Trust me. This is all going to blow over."

"You'd better be right, Gilmore. Everything started out so well. I never imagined that anything would go wrong. If only Worth hadn't gone nosing into stuff that was none of his business, we wouldn't have had to get rid of him."

"You mean you're the one who wouldn't have had to get rid of him," Gilmore amended. "I had nothing to do with that."

"Then there was Peacock snooping around trying to

find out who killed his friend," he went on just as if Gilmore hadn't spoken a word.

Gilmore fished a cigar from his humidor and clipped the end. "You've heard that old Scottish saying about the best laid schemes going astray. In any plan, it's wise to make room for adjustments."

Lange glared at him. "Since when did you become a philosopher—or a tactician?"

Gilmore struck a match. "I'm just pointing out the obvious, that's all."

"Hmmph," said Lange, glaring across at the man who was becoming more irritating by the moment.

"Help yourself to a cigar," Gilmore invited.

"Nope," said Lange, rising from his chair. "I think I'll go have that drink now."

Luke was on his way to the jail when he heard his name called softly. It was coming from the corner of the mercantile. Warily, he stepped over to the space between the mercantile and the café. The gossipy old man Jubal Bench was lurking there.

"Is there something you wanted?" he asked, recalling that it was Bench who'd carried news of his arrival to Dewitt.

"I like that Lily Peacock," he said. "She's a good woman. She's fed me more'n once when I was down on my luck."

Luke nodded. "Go on," he encouraged.

"Well, of late, I've seen that storekeeper Bledsoe sneaking out of town in the middle of the night. I kind of like to keep an eye on things, you see. He's gone out three times that I know of. I don't know when he gets back, but the store is always open the next morning. When I've gone inside, he looks like he ain't getting much sleep."

"That's interesting. Which direction does he go?"

"He headed out east out of town. After that, I don't know."

A couple of things crossed Luke's mind. Bledsoe might be one of the cattle rustlers. Still, he didn't seem the type, and rustling wasn't done on a schedule. The other possibility gave him hope for Russ Peacock. Bledsoe might be holding him prisoner somewhere. Obviously the same thing had occurred to Bench. But why not simply kill Peacock?

"Do you know when Bledsoe is due to make his next trip?" he asked.

"I expect it to be tonight. He always goes right after it gets dark. He thinks he's sneaking away without anybody noticing."

Luke wondered if the other council members were aware of Bledsoe's nocturnal rides across country. Likely not, he decided. He shook the old man's hand.

"Thanks for telling me this, Jubal. If you learn anything else, let me know. But be careful. Coffer got beat up simply because I took my horses and mule to the livery stable and was passing the time of day with him."

"I heard. I never much liked that Dewitt, nor Morgan either. Both of 'em has got a mean streak. I'm not the only one who's glad they're locked up. You be careful, Marshal."

Luke stayed to watch the old man edge his way down to the alley until he disappeared around the corner. Then he stepped back onto the boardwalk and headed for the jail, where Morgan and his sidekick were complaining loudly from their cells. Fahl was sitting at the desk with a shotgun across his knees, blithely ignoring the ruckus.

"How are things going?" said Luke, commandeering a chair opposite.

"Fine and dandy. Ham is going around to the businesses to let folks know that we're the law in Braxton now. Though I expect most of 'em already know it. We had ourselves an audience when we arrested those two, and word gets around fast."

"Do you think you and Isham can handle things here in town for a while?"

"I reckon so. What is it you have in mind to do?"

"It may be a wild goose chase, but I think Russ Peacock might still be alive. I suspect he's being held prisoner somewhere. Anyway, Bledsoe sneaks out of town at regular intervals. He might be riding out to check on him, taking him food and whatnot. I'm going to see if I can pick up his trail."

"I sure hope you're right about Peacock being alive," said Fahl. "I'd offer to go with you, but Ham needs me here. No telling what kind of trouble that fancy-pants banker is going to start."

"Don't worry, I can handle this myself. But first off, I'm going to stop at the café and pick up some grub to take along."

"Are you planning to tell Miss Lily what you suspect about her father?"

"No. I considered it, but I don't want to get her hopes up. I might be wrong."

"Probably best," he agreed.

Luke left Fahl to his job of guarding the prisoners and stepped outside. His next stop was the café, where he picked up some tortillas stuffed with smoked venison. He exchanged a few words with Lily, who still looked anxious, but he kept the purpose of his mission to himself. After telling Coffer where he was headed, he mounted up and rode out of town.

He hadn't gone more than a couple of miles before he spotted a set of tracks veering off the trail and heading north. The wind had played havoc with most of them, but there was still enough in the sheltered spots to lead him on. He was becoming more and more hopeful that his hunch was right and Russ Peacock was alive. He wanted to find the place, free the prisoner, and wait for Bledsoe to arrive.

The tracks led ever northward through spiky yuccas and clumps of mesquite. He checked his back trail often to see if he was being followed. Clouds were forming over the mountain peaks. If it rained on the flats, it would wipe out all signs, and Bledsoe's trail would be lost.

The merchant's horse had moved into the foothills. At this higher elevation, the land was thickly dotted with stubby piñon pines and junipers. The ground was broken and strewn with boulders. It was a perfect place for a hideout.

Luke paused to don his waterproof poncho. He was none too soon, for the storm that was threatening broke suddenly.

He lowered the brim of his hat to protect his face from the downpour and rode on, searching to find a clue as to where a prisoner might be held. He was almost on top of the shack before he saw it. It was wedged in among boulders and scrub and hard to see unless you were looking for it. He tethered his horse beneath a rock overhang and eased his way across to the shack. It appeared to be deserted, and there was a bar in place across the door. The windowless structure made an effective prison. He removed the bar and called out Peacock's name.

"Help me" was the weak response.

Luke yanked the door open wide and went inside. The prisoner had been wounded and was lying on a pallet in one corner. There was a makeshift bandage around one shoulder, and it was stained with blood. The room was hot and airless.

"You must be Russ Peacock," he said to the sandy-haired man who was stretched out before him.

"Yeah. Who are you?"

"Marshal Eastburn sent me. I'm Luke Cochran, his deputy."

"Thank goodness," he said, trying to rise by leaning on his good arm. "I was bushwhacked on my way to see my friend McDougal. It was Lange, the banker, who shot me. He thought I was dead, but he ordered Hiram Bledsoe to put another bullet in me to make sure. I heard him, plain as day. I'd just been at Bledsoe's store. Guess he'd left the place in the care of his helper so he could join his partner."

"What happened then?" said Luke.

"Lange headed back to town, leaving Bledsoe to carry out his order. Lucky for me, Bledsoe's not a killer. He fired into the air and then he hauled me up here to this place. I've been his prisoner ever since. He brings me food and water and changes my bandage, but he won't let me go. Says that Lange would kill him and me both."

Luke helped Peacock to his feet.

"You need to get out of here and breathe some fresh air."

The wounded man leaned heavily on Luke's arm, and they went outside. Peacock lifted his face to feel the cooling effect of the raindrops as they washed over him. There was just enough time for him to get soaked before the rain eased off and the clouds moved on.

"How did you find me, Marshal?" Peacock asked.

"I got a tip that Bledsoe was sneaking out of town at night. I followed the tracks as far as I could, and then I stumbled onto this shack."

"I owe a debt to whoever tipped you off. I've been worried about my daughter. How is she?"

"Lily's fine. She's worried about you, but she's doing a good job running the café in your absence."

Luke eased Peacock into a sitting position on a rock.

"If you think you can hang on, I'd like to stick around and wait for Bledsoe. I understand he has a visit scheduled for tonight."

"I'll make it all right. Besides, I'd like to see his face when he finds the shack is empty."

"For sure, he can't deny his involvement in what was done to you. Maybe we can get him to talk."

"I'm grateful to him for not shooting me," said Peacock, "and for bringing me food and water. But I had a miserable time of it locked in that hot, airless shed without a doctor's attention. If you hadn't found me, I think I would have died. Could be that's what Bledsoe was hoping for."

Luke could tell that Peacock was in a lot of pain and had been for a long time.

"Wait here," he said. "I'll be back in a minute."

He retraced his steps to the overhang where the bay was tied, opened a saddlebag, and fished around until he came up with the bottle he was looking for. It was his own emergency supply of laudanum. Unlike Hatch, however, Luke used it the proper way, only when needed. Again he reached inside the saddlebag. This time he pulled out a Smith & Wesson revolver that had belonged to his father. He set the bottle aside and loaded the gun. When he got back, he handed the bottle to the wounded man.

"Take some of this," he said.

Peacock recognized the bottle and took a dose of its contents gratefully.

"Better have this too," Luke said, handing over the revolver. "Chances are, you'll need it."

Peacock hefted it. "Thanks for both," he said, "though I'll return the gun when I can get one of my own."

It wasn't long before the medicine took effect and Peacock's pain began to ease. Luke fetched the pallet from the shed and spread it in the shade of some junipers for Peacock to rest on. The sun dried Luke's clothes as they waited. When it started slipping below the horizon, it painted the sky in shades of red and orange.

"A pretty sight," said Peacock. "I was afraid it was one I'd never see again."

Luke didn't voice his thought that if left to Lange, the councilman would already have seen his final sunset.

The last of the light slowly faded as the stars appeared. It was a sight that Luke never tired of.

When the darkness had deepened, he figured that Bledsoe had left Braxton and was on his way. While they waited, Luke filled Peacock in on what had been happening in town during his absence.

"Well, Marshal, I have to say that I'm glad you jailed Morgan and that dumb cluck he's got for a deputy."

When Luke told him about Coffer's beating, he could scarcely believe it.

"They ought to have the same thing done to them," he said.

"The beating might have been Morgan's idea, but he was hired by the council and kept on by them. To my way of thinking, the other council members are just as responsible for what happened, especially Lange."

"I've got to agree," he said sadly. "They're all crooks. You made good choices with Isham and Fahl, though. They're both fine men. I only wish they would wear badges permanently."

So did Luke, although he doubted that either man felt a calling for law enforcement.

"Maybe you'll be able to persuade them when this mess is cleaned up," he said, "but right now they're only on loan from Lyman Berry."

From the time the sun went down, it grew steadily colder. Luke slipped back to the bay to retrieve his coat along with a blanket for Peacock, who was shivering. The man was already weak from blood loss and couldn't afford to get sick from exposure. Luke moved the bay a little farther away so Bledsoe's horse wouldn't get wind of him and warn his rider.

Once they were garbed against the cold and sheltered on the lee side of a boulder, Luke was able to wait with greater patience. Peacock, on the other hand, was more like a racehorse at the starting line. He wanted action. He was anxious to confront the man who'd kept him locked up, wounded as he was, in that cramped, airless prison all those painful days.

"Bledsoe is a frightened man," said Luke softly. "He's jumping at his own shadow. The way I've got it figured, Lange and Gilmore have something on him, something that keeps him in line and keeps him following orders. You're lucky he didn't have the meanness in him to follow Lange's order and shoot you again. He took a risk to save you."

"I guess so," said Peacock. "Still, it's hard for me to think kindly of him. I once considered him a friend of sorts."

"Maybe, in his own limited way, he was trying to be a friend to you when you were wounded, but he was caught between a rock and a hard place. I doubt if he knew what else to do."

Another dose of laudanum eased Peacock's pain enough for him to nod off. Luke figured the man needed the rest and kept his vigil alone. In the quiet of the night, he thought about what had happened since he'd ridden into town. He needed a plan of action, one that would put Lange and his partners on the defensive. His first step had been to swear in two deputies and arrest Morgan and Dewitt. But it was time for the next step.

Luke had been sitting in one position for so long that the muscles in his legs began to cramp. He got up and walked around to ease them. It was then that he heard the faint clink of a horseshoe on shelf rock. He hurried over and shook Peacock awake.

"He's coming," he whispered. "Be ready."

They could hear Bledsoe dismount a short distance from the shack. They waited while he walked the rest of the way on foot. By moonlight, they could see him reach the front door. When he started to lift the bar that had been replaced, Luke stepped from the shadows. Gun in hand, he disarmed the storekeeper.

"Please don't shoot," Bledsoe begged. "I'm here on an errand of mercy."

"I know all about your mercy," said Luke. "Aren't you worried that Lange will find out that your friend Peacock is alive?"

"Yeah," said Peacock, who'd come up beside him. "Were you saving me until you found someone with the guts to kill me?"

"No, I swear," he said, his voice rising. "I never wanted to hurt you. I never wanted anyone to hurt you."

"We're going to believe you—for now," said Luke.

"How did you find out about this place?" said Bledsoe. "I didn't think anyone knew about it. Not even Lange, who thinks he knows everything."

"Let's just say that your nighttime trips weren't as big a secret as you imagined them to be."

In the moonlight, Luke could see the man's body tremble. He was scared to death, both of Lange and of the law.

"Look, if I hadn't brought Russ here, he'd be dead by now," he said, as if arguing in court for leniency.

"I'll admit it," said Peacock. "Still, Hiram, you're on the wrong side of the law."

Luke took a minute to check Bledsoe for hidden weapons. The gun was all he was carrying.

"Now what do you imagine will happen when I ride into Braxton with you and Peacock beside me?" Luke asked.

"Please don't do that," Bledsoe begged. "It would be a death sentence, and all because I refused to kill a friend."

Luke felt sorry for him. There was a lot to what he said. He could tell that Peacock was feeling pity for him too.

While he waited for the storekeeper's return, Luke had formed a plan. Maybe if Bledsoe had a long, unexplained absence from Braxton, it would rattle Lange and the others. Make them worry a little. Maybe it would worry them enough to cause them to make a mistake.

Chapter Seven

Luke waited for daylight before heading out of the foothills. Russ Peacock was weak from blood loss, but he was game. He rode double with Bledsoe, for his own horse had disappeared at the time he was shot. The store-keeper was as scared as a man facing the gallows. Luke decided to reassure him.

"I'm not taking you to Braxton," he said. "We both know that wouldn't be a wise thing to do."

He saw some of the tension drain away from the man's posture.

"Lange would kill me before the sun set," Bledsoe agreed. "He's a vindictive animal who cares for nothing but power and money."

Luke didn't need persuading. In his opinion, Lange was a rattlesnake.

"Where are we taking him, then?" said Peacock. "I want to see my daughter. I want her to know that I'm still alive."

"We're going to McDougal's place. He'll be safe there

S. J. Stewart

for the time being, and so will you. I'll send the doc out to tend your wound when I get back to town, and I'll get word to Lily that you're all right."

"What about Hiram's store?" said Peacock. "Won't people wonder what's happened to him? He's not the type to change his routine."

"That's true," said the storekeeper, "but it can't be helped. I can't go back to town. Not now."

"I'm counting on Lange and Gilmore to notice that the store is closed," said Luke. "I want them to worry."

"You mean you're not going back and arresting Lange for attempted murder?" said Peacock.

"Look, all I've got is yours and Bledsoe's testimony. You'd both have to come in and give it in order for me to arrest him. When you did, you'd both become targets."

Peacock thought about that. "Guess you're right, Marshal. I'll bide my time."

Luke stopped to give the horses a breather. Bledsoe's mount needed one, for it was carrying a double load. Peacock looked like he needed to stop and rest from time to time as well. Blood loss had made him pale and weak. While they were stopped, Luke gave him the last of the laudanum.

"I sure hope Harry and Charlie have some of this stuff on hand," he said before swallowing the last of the contents in a single gulp.

Luke hoped so too.

Charlie was watching when they rode in. Upon seeing that Peacock was wounded, he ran out to help ease him from the saddle.

"It's Russ," he called out to McDougal. "He's alive, though he don't look to be in any too good a shape."

The old rancher and Louisa came rushing out. Luke and McDougal helped the wounded man to the house, while Charlie led the horses to the barn. Louisa, clucking like a mother hen, hurried on ahead to fetch bandages and alcohol. Bledsoe followed behind the others like an orphan child who wasn't quite sure of his welcome.

After Peacock had been washed, his wound cleaned and freshly bandaged, and his dirty clothes changed for one of McDougal's nightshirts that smelled of sunshine and fresh air, he was put to bed.

All the while, Bledsoe stood gazing out the front window. Luke wondered how someone of his temperament had gotten mixed up with the likes of Lange and Gilmore. Whatever had brought them together had been sorry luck for the storekeeper.

He was convinced that Lange had a past, one that fit on a wanted poster. But it was up to Eastburn to expose that past. He decided that he'd make another trip to Parsons as soon as possible to learn what his boss had ferreted out.

After Peacock had been made comfortable and was thinking more clearly, Luke entered the bedroom to question him again. He asked Bledsoe to accompany him, and they stood at the foot of the bed.

While Peacock owed the storekeeper his life, his feelings for his former jailer weren't all that friendly. There was a lot of awkwardness.

"Lange ordered me to go along when he set out to bushwhack you," said Bledsoe, making a stab at justifying his behavior. "I had no choice. I left my helper to mind the store and met Lange outside of town. We both knew you were coming here to McDougal's, for you'd just been in to buy peppermints. We were able to get ahead and find a hiding place because you stopped and spent some time at the café before riding out of town."

He turned to Luke and continued his story.

"Lange and I hid in a wash near the trail. When Russ appeared, we kept quiet. After he'd gone on past, Lange raised up out of that wash and shot him in the back. It's a lucky thing the bullet missed the vitals."

"Then what happened?" Luke encouraged.

"Lange assumed that Russ was dead, since he was lying on the ground so still. And he's conceited. He thinks that everything he does is right near perfect. Still, just because he knew that Russ and me were friendly, he ordered me to go over and put a bullet in him to make sure."

To Luke's way of thinking, Lange deserved a rope more than most who were hung.

"Why did you have to haul me off to that shack and lock me up?" Peacock demanded to know.

"I couldn't let you go back to town after I'd been ordered to put a bullet in you. I couldn't take you anywhere else either. Leastwise, not where there were people. Word would have gotten around. Then we would both be dead men."

"So you were just going to leave me there to die slow and miserable."

Bledsoe hung his head. "I admit it wasn't the best solution, but it was the only one I could come up with. I was just plain scared."

"I'm wondering how you got mixed up with Lange in the first place," said Luke. "And what kind of hold does he have on you that is so strong he can make you do things you don't want to do?"

"I sure didn't want to get mixed up with Lange, and it wasn't my idea. I settled in and was doing just fine with the store. Then Lange showed up to establish a bank. It wasn't long before he recognized me from Kansas. Back there, they claimed I'd killed a man who'd tried to cheat me in a business deal. I was innocent, but they sentenced me to hang. It was the real killer who busted me out of jail and got me away from there. He was the dead man's brother-in-law. He'd killed his sister's husband because the bully had beaten her—more than once. The last time her husband beat her, her brother cornered the no-account in his barn and shot him. Told me it was like getting rid of a mad dog, but he didn't want an innocent man to hang for it. Unfortunately, Lange was in the area at the time and he heard about it. Worse, he'd seen me."

"So he was blackmailing you in order to make you part of his scheme," said Luke. "I suspected it had to be something like that."

"That explains a lot," said Peacock. "I heard tell you took more'n one box of groceries to the widow Cannon after her husband died and the widow and her children were left in a bad way. Fact is, I've heard of several acts of kindness you've performed. You're no killer. You've just been saddled with bad company."

Bledsoe looked grateful for Peacock's change of heart.

Louisa appeared in the doorway. "The flapjacks and coffee are ready," she said. "I'll bring you a tray, Señor Russ. The rest of you, go to the table."

Luke was ravenous, and the coffee and golden brown flapjacks smelled like heaven.

After the meal, he thanked Louisa and made ready to leave.

He turned to Bledsoe. "Stay put," he ordered. "I want Lange and his partners to worry. If they think you've run out on them, they might tip their hand."

"I'm not about to miss out on Louisa's cooking," he said, "and nothing could make me go into town."

"I'll send Dr. Vanhelden out as soon as I get there," he promised. "If anyone gets curious, I'll say that McDougal's stomach started acting up."

"That should work," said Charlie.

Luke went to the bedroom to tell Peacock he was leaving.

"You won't forget to let my daughter know that I'm all right?" he said.

"I'll make that a priority."

Outside, he found that his horse had been curried and grained by one of the hired hands. He waved his thanks to Charlie as he rode out.

It was late that evening when he got back to town. The stars were out, and the moon was creeping around a cloud. It struck him immediately that something wasn't right. For one thing, there was no light on in the jail. For another, there was lots of light and activity at the undertaker's establishment. Instead of going directly to Lily's place and giving her the good news about her father, he headed for the jail. His first concern was his deputies. He paused and listened before going inside.

"Anybody there?" he called out softly from the side

of the door, remembering Morgan's shattering shotgun blast.

"Come on in" came Fahl's voice from the darkness.

Luke stepped inside. The place had a coppery smell, like that of spilt blood.

Something had happened.

"Is there a reason you doused the light?"

"Yep. Somebody shot through the bars and killed Morgan deader than old John Calhoun. Whoever it was, he killed Dewitt too. I don't care to make myself a target."

One name leaped to Luke's mind: Hobart Lange.

"I found out that Lange tried to kill Peacock," Luke said. "He shot him in the back when he was on his way to McDougal's. Morgan had to know about this. When he was jailed, Lange must have been afraid he would talk. Dewitt was a liability too."

"So Russ is alive?" said Fahl, a note of hope in his voice.

"Yes. Bledsoe took him to a shack in the foothills and was doctoring him as best he could. The bullet went through clean and didn't hit any vitals. The storekeeper was blackmailed into helping Lange, but when Lange ordered him to finish Peacock off, he didn't. Saved his life instead."

"I'll be. That's the best news I've heard all day. I know Miss Lily is going to be relieved to hear that her father's alive. You bring him and Bledsoe to town?"

"No. I don't think Braxton is too healthy for either of them right now. They're both at the McDougal ranch. I expect they'll be safe there for the time being."

"Safest place around, I'd guess. Those two old men are salty."

"I need to find Lily and tell her the good news. Then I'll send Vanhelden out to the ranch to take a look at her father's wound. After that's done, I'm riding to Parsons. My boss has been looking into Lange's past. When I get back, depending on the findings, I may be able to arrest him."

"You be careful, amigo. Lange was asking around town about you. He's over at the Lucky Horseshoe right now, having a powwow with Gilmore. Hatch is busy as an ant at a church picnic over at his place, what with those two bodies to take care of."

"Where's Isham?"

"He's out patrolling the streets. The killings have made a lot of people nervous, and the sight of a badge tends to calm them down some."

"Well, since everybody's occupied, I might be able to get out of town without being noticed. If you wouldn't mind, it'd be a help if you'd tell Lily that her father has been found alive."

"Be glad to," said Fahl. "It'd pleasure me to deliver good news for once. As soon as Ham gets back, I'll do it."

"Tell her it's important that she keep quiet about it and not let on that anything is different."

"I'll tell her."

"Then I'll dispatch Vanhelden to the ranch and be on my way. Hold the fort."

"It's what I do best," said Fahl.

The doctor was in his living quarters at the back. Luke filled him in on what had happened.

"Thank heaven that killer didn't succeed," Vanhelden said. "Miss Lily needs her father. I'll head out to see Russ first thing in the morning, but luckily Louisa is a right fair doctor herself."

Luke's next stop was the livery stable. Coffer had gone home, and the place was empty. He switched his tack to the dun. After rubbing down the bay and feeding it some oats, he was ready to go. Leaving Braxton in the hands of his deputies, he pointed his horse's nose toward Parsons.

He'd spent a mostly sleepless night and two long days in the saddle. He ached for a hot meal and a warm bed. But, even more, he wanted to know whom he was dealing with. Where had Lange come from? What had he been in a past life?

Once he was well away from town, he stopped and made camp under a canopy of stars. He was scarcely into his blankets when he fell into an exhausted sleep. The sun was peeking over the horizon when something caused Luke to come fully awake. He paused a moment to listen, trying to recall what it was that had disturbed his sleep. Then he heard the dun nicker a warning and saw its ears twitch. Someone was close by. He rolled from his blankets, grabbing the rifle he'd kept by his side. An instant later a bullet slammed into the place where his head had just been.

He crouched behind a mesquite bush, making himself as small a target as possible. The sniper was hidden in a nearby arroyo. This was the same way Lange had gotten a bullet into Peacock. Luke could see the top of the man's hat, his arm, and a rifle barrel. He swung up his own rifle and fired. What little he could see of the shooter disappeared.

He listened for any sound that might give his enemy away. Then he heard hoofbeats running toward the west. The sniper had called it quits. He raced to the arroyo, hoping to identify his would-be killer. In the distance, he could see the back of the retreating outlaw. He wore a nondescript duster and rode an equally nondescript horse. No doubt there were a dozen horses in Braxton just like it, and at least as many tan dusters. It could have been Lange or Gilmore, either one, or somebody they'd enlisted to do their dirty work for them.

There was no use trying to catch him, for he had too much of a lead. Anyway, Luke didn't want to be drawn away from his business in Parsons. Hopefully, there would be a wire telling him the identity and past crimes of the Braxton banker, and maybe some others besides.

He muttered under his breath when he rolled up a blanket that now sported a bullet hole. *Don't bellyache*, he told himself. *An instant sooner and that bullet would have gone through your head.*

During the rest of the trip to Parsons, he thought about who the sniper might have been. The meeting between Lange and Gilmore could have ended and either one could have spotted him leaving town. Then too, maybe Hatch hadn't been as busy at the funeral parlor as it appeared.

When Luke rode into town, he went straight to the telegraph office. The telegrapher looked up and recognized him. "Your wire came yesterday," he said. "Long as it is, it must have cost a small fortune to send."

"Could I see it?" said Luke, not bothering to keep the impatience out of his voice.

"Sure," he said, fumbling through a stack of papers. "Here it is."

Luke took it and scanned it quickly. Then he read it through again.

LANGE WANTED IN KANSAS FOR MURDER OF BANK TELLER (STOP) EMBEZZLEMENT (STOP) REAL NAME HANK MOSEMAN (STOP) GILMORE A CONMAN FROM NEW ORLEANS (STOP) BLEDSOE WANTED IN KANSAS FOR MURDER (STOP) REAL NAME SHELBY BROOKS (STOP) HATCH BELIEVED TO BE MOSEMAN'S PARTNER (STOP) REAL NAME MORT RIGBY (STOP) CONVICTED OF MURDERING SEVERAL YOUNG WOMEN (STOP) ESCAPED JAIL (STOP)

"Looks like you've got trouble," said the telegrapher, who was well aware of the telegram's contents.

"That's nothing new," said Luke, as he stuffed the paper into his pocket and stepped outside.

Before leaving town, he stopped by the jail to have a word with his friend Pete.

"It sounds like you've got 'em worried," said the Parsons lawman when Luke told him about the sniper. "Somebody's keeping a close eye on you."

"Well, whoever it was, I ran him off. Still, that doesn't mean he won't circle around and wait to ambush me."

"You could stick around until nightfall. It'd make you a lot harder target."

"No. Instead of going back to town, I'm heading straight for McDougal's. I want to tell him and Peacock what this wire says about their town council."

"Then good luck—and be careful."

As he rode out of Parsons, Luke thought about luck. One thing he'd noticed was its flightiness. Sometimes good luck flew in and lit on a man's shoulder. Other times it stayed far away like a fellow had a contagious disease or something. He admitted that he'd had his share, though, and he hoped for more, because sometimes being careful simply wasn't enough.

Chapter Eight

Lange was in full voice as he paced back and forth in front of Gilmore's desk. He was past caring whether or not he was overheard. Gilmore sat quietly, trying to block Lange's tirade from his consciousness, hiding everything he felt in a poker face that he'd perfected over the years on riverboats and saloons from Colorado to the Mississippi.

"I'll kill that little weasel when I find him," Lange ranted. "He knows way too much, and he'll spill his guts the first time anyone raises a hand to him."

"You don't know for sure that he's gone into hiding or sneaked out of the country," said Gilmore when Lange paused for breath. "He hasn't been gone that long."

Lange glowered. "Since when did Bledsoe fail to open the store at eight o'clock sharp? It's like a religion to him. You know how he has to do the same things at the same time."

Lange had a point. Bledsoe was a man of habit, and

any deviation was a sign that something serious had prevented him from following his routine.

"Did you check his house? Maybe he fell and broke something or maybe he's sick."

"That's the first thing I did. His horse is gone. He sneaked off last night, and he hasn't come back."

Gilmore hadn't been to the mercantile, and he hadn't seen Bledsoe since Cochran had arrived. He was as uneasy as Lange about the marshal's sudden appearance and all the snooping around he'd been doing. When Cochran had sworn in two deputies and jailed Morgan and Dewitt, his anxiety escalated. He imagined that Bledsoe must be scared witless. Maybe he was scared enough to leave everything he'd worked for behind and make a run for it.

"We've got to find him," said Lange, "and I can't be away from the bank. My absence would be noticed."

"So you're saying it's up to me to go out and look for him?"

"That's exactly what I'm saying."

It took all the self-restraint Gilmore could muster to keep from blowing up in Lange's face. "Look, I don't care where Bledsoe ran off to," Gilmore said with calm finality. "Anything he says to the law will only implicate himself. He'll keep quiet. Trust me. Chances are, he'll be back as soon as he gets his nerves under control."

Lange looked somewhat mollified. "Maybe you're right," he agreed. "But I'm sick and tired of mollycoddling that spineless excuse for a man."

"Then you're better off if he doesn't return."

"Possibly. It's just that I can't trust him to keep his mouth shut if he's the least bit pressured."

Lange was making it clear that he'd feel better with Bledsoe dead, maybe for more than one reason. In addition to shutting him up permanently, with Bledsoe out of the way it would mean one less man to divide the spoils with. In the beginning there was to have been a six-way split. Now that Morgan and Dewitt were dead, the split was down to four. If Bledsoe were to disappear permanently, he'd forfeit his share of a fortune, and it would be divided three ways.

Gilmore wondered what could have caused the storekeeper to ride out of town during the night and not return. He doubted the reason was a case of nerves. If Lange wasn't so upset, Gilmore would suspect that Lange had already gotten rid of Bledsoe.

"Are you listening to me?" Lange demanded, sensing that Gilmore's attention had wandered.

"Yes. I was just thinking. Bledsoe's not going to run out on all the money that's coming to him. The promise of wealth gives a man a pretty strong backbone, even a man like him. I wonder if something could have happened."

"I still think you should saddle up and go looking for him. Follow his tracks and see where he headed."

This was a thinly veiled order. Beneath his desk, where Lange couldn't see, Gilmore clenched and unclenched his fists to keep his temper under control.

"I'm a gambler, not a tracker," Gilmore said coldly. "If you want him followed, you're going to have to get one of those rustlers you hired to do it."

Lange stopped pacing and faced him straight on. "I would, but they're all out at the Barton place, and I've got to get back to the bank and see to a foreclosure."

Gilmore felt a tremor of disgust. While he fancied that

he was a better than average con artist who'd begun his career by cheating at cards, he couldn't understand the pleasure Lange derived from foreclosures. The banker wasn't taking a few thousand dollars from inept gamblers or greedy investors; he was robbing families of the homes they'd worked hard to build. First he stole their cattle until they were broke, and then he seized their ranches. Gilmore tried to shrug away a mental reminder that he was sharing in those same profits. Money did strange things to a man's conscience, he observed.

After what had happened to Morgan and Dewitt, not to mention Mayor Worth and Peacock, Gilmore figured it would be a good idea to watch his back. There was no end to Lange's greed, and the man didn't know the meaning of loyalty.

"I guess I can't count on you for any help," said Lange, giving him a look of disgust as he started to leave.

"Like I said, I'm a gambler, not a tracker."

Lange left, slamming the door behind him.

Luke was watchful as he rode across the high plain toward McDougal's ranch. He took care to avoid places that would make a good bushwhacker's lair. When he got back to town, he'd ask Isham and Fahl if they'd noticed anyone's absence after he'd left. The sniper who'd tried to kill him must have watched him go.

He hoped that his two deputies weren't having any trouble. The way it looked, though, the townspeople were mighty glad to have them.

The close call he'd had weighed on him. Close calls always did. He thought of his young son, Gareth, so far away. He wanted to be an important part of Gareth's life, to teach him things, to go fishing with him. That sniper's bullet came close to robbing him of the chance to be a proper father.

When Eastburn sent him down to Braxton to investigate Worth's murder and to look into the problem of widespread rustling, he'd followed orders because it was his job. Now he had a personal interest as well. He was going to hunt down the man who had tried to kill him.

When he rode into the yard of the ranch house, Charlie was waiting for him.

"I saw you coming," he said. "Didn't expect you back here so soon, though."

"I've been over to Parsons. I went to pick up a wire from my boss and thought you'd like to know what it said."

The old man looked at him expectantly. "Well, I reckon so. The ones in the house will want to hear too."

He turned and led the way, calling out to a young boy who was leading a couple of mules toward the barn.

"Come, Tobias, and take care of the marshal's horse. We've got important business to discuss in the house."

"Si, señor," said the boy. "I will take good care of him."

"How's Bledsoe behaving?" asked Luke.

"As good as can be. He's scared his pals will find him. Convinced that Lange will shoot him on sight."

"I expect he knows Lange as well as anybody."

Louisa was pleased to welcome Luke and hurried about the kitchen fixing something for him to eat.

McDougal took him into the big front room and invited him to be seated on one of the cowhide-covered chairs. Peacock and Bledsoe joined them. Peacock appeared a whole lot better than when Luke last saw him.

Bledsoe didn't. He had a drawn and frightened look about him.

"The doctor came out to see me," said Peacock when Luke asked how he was. "But he couldn't improve on what Louisa had already done."

"Don't let her hear that," said McDougal. "It'll give her the big head. We can't have that. She'll ask for more money."

"I will ask for a raise anyway," she said, coming to the doorway with a big grin on her face. "It is good to be appreciated for a change, Señor Peacock."

"I appreciate you every time I sit down for a meal," said McDougal. "A plate that's wiped clean should say it all."

Luke sat patiently through the banter.

"Now, what's on your mind, Marshal?" said McDougal as soon as Louisa went back to her work.

"I know who the Braxton council members really are. Marshal Eastburn sent me a wire."

He noticed Bledsoe tense up.

"Well, go on," said Peacock impatiently. "Who are they?"

"Lange's real name is Hank Moseman. He embezzled money from a Kansas bank and killed a bank teller who was on to him. I expect they want him in Lyon County real bad."

"Did you know that?" Peacock asked Bledsoe.

"I knew he was from Kansas because he'd read of my trouble, but I didn't know he was in trouble himself."

"What about the others?" said Peacock.

"Hatch's name is Mort Rigby. He's wanted in Texas for killing five women. I can't tell you any more because

Eastburn is tightfisted with his money—too tightfisted to send me a lot of details in a telegram."

"And what about Gilmore?" McDougal prompted.

"He didn't change his name, and he's apparently not wanted for anything. But he's got a reputation for being a con artist."

"I guess you know that my name is Shelby Brooks," said Bledsoe. "Like I told you, I was falsely accused of murder and sentenced to hang. The real killer helped me to escape. I was trying to start over and make a decent life for myself when Lange happened by and started blackmailing me. I didn't have any choice but to go along. It was that or be hung for a killing I didn't do."

"He did save my bacon by hauling me off to that shack instead of shooting me," said Peacock. "I think that's a big point in Hiram's favor."

Luke had to agree, though it couldn't have done Peacock any good being locked up and left alone when he'd needed medical attention. A man less strong and healthy could have died.

"Did you tell my daughter that I'm still alive?" said Peacock.

"Afraid I delegated that pleasant chore to Homer Fahl because I needed to get on the trail to Parsons as soon as possible. I left in the night, but somebody was watching and saw me go. I was bushwhacked the next morning at dawn. Only a stroke of luck saved me from being killed."

"Somebody's getting worried," said McDougal. "What do you plan to do now, Marshal?"

"I'm going to ride into Braxton and worry them some more."

"I'm riding along with you," said Peacock. "I want to see my daughter, and I've got a business to run."

"Lange tried to kill you once, my friend," said McDougal. "Do you think he would hesitate to try again?"

"I don't believe Lange would risk shooting him down in the middle of the street," said Luke. "Besides, it's time to go on the offensive."

"Don't tell them where I am," pleaded Bledsoe. "Lange is the worst, but I don't trust the other two either. Lange's got a bunch of outlaws working for him that he can call in to do his dirty work whenever he wants to."

"Do you know where they're hiding out?" asked Luke.

"I'm not sure, but Lange was anxious to foreclose on the Barton ranch. It was the first one he took over, and I think he wanted it for a hideout."

Peacock explained where the Barton ranch was located.

"We'll leave that trip for later," said Luke. "Right now I want to get back to Braxton and put the pressure on."

"Are you going to walk right up and arrest Lange?" said McDougal.

"That depends. I'll have to wait and see."

"Well, don't underestimate any of them," the rancher warned. "Lange, for one, isn't going to give up easy."

Luke didn't expect for one minute that he would.

Chapter Nine

Luke's arrival in town, with Russ Peacock riding beside him, caused a considerable stir. Those on the street ducked inside to tell others. Quickly the crowd of onlookers grew. A young fellow in a boiled shirt and string tie pushed his way through the crowd and headed straight toward them. He had a pad of paper clutched in one hand and a pencil stuck behind his ear.

"Uh-oh, here comes Niles Sinclair, the newspaperman," said Peacock. "It looks like I'm going to be making the next edition of the *Braxton Bugle*."

Luke had planned to talk to him, but now wasn't the time.

Sinclair walked into the street and stood in front of the horses. Luke had to either stop or run him down.

"Mr. Peacock," said Sinclair, "why did you go off and disappear the way you did? You must know that your daughter and your friends have all been worried sick about you."

He made it sound like Peacock had sneaked off on his

own. This didn't sit well with the council member. He didn't try to hide his annoyance at the newspaperman's insinuation.

"Listen here, Sinclair, I was bushwhacked and left for dead. Then I was taken to a shack in the foothills. I was a prisoner there until the marshal rescued me."

"That's quite a story. Did you see who shot you?"

"Yes," said Peacock, his answer terse.

"Would you care to share that information?"

"Nope. Not now. Not with you."

"Well, at least tell me who took you to that shack and kept you prisoner there."

"Be glad to. It was Hiram Bledsoe."

Sinclair's expression was one of shocked disbelief. There was also a collective gasp from the onlookers who'd been listening.

"Why isn't Mr. Bledsoe with you then? And why would he do such a thing?"

"We didn't bring him along," said Luke. "He's someplace where nobody can find him. That was my advice and his choice. The reasons are apt to come to light soon."

Just then he saw Lily running from the café to greet her father. Peacock climbed down from the horse and gave her a bear hug. Luke saw him wince in pain.

"You're hurt," she said. "You need to see the doctor."

"Already seen him," Peacock said softly so no one besides Luke and Lily could hear, except maybe Sinclair.

"I've got to go with the marshal to the jail," he said. "I'll be home directly."

"I'm coming with you," she said, reluctant to let go of him. "You're to tell me everything that happened to you, down to the last detail."

Peacock glanced up at Luke, silently asking permission for his daughter to join them.

"Bring her along," he said. "She deserves to know."

Lily shot him a look of gratitude and kept her place beside her father, who was leading his mount. Sinclair started to follow along but Luke waved him off.

"Marshal, the people of Braxton have a right to know what's going on," he protested. "There has been too much lawlessness."

"You're obstructing my investigation," said Luke, glaring at the reporter. "Keep on and I'll lock you up."

Sinclair backed off.

On the way to the jail, Luke kept an eye on the crowd, searching for any sign of Gilmore or Hatch.

His two deputies were waiting for him when he arrived with the Peacocks.

"Russ, it's sure good to see you, my friend," said Fahl, who reached out to shake his hand. Isham pulled out a chair for Lily.

Luke dropped the bar across the door in case the reporter or anyone else got bold enough to intrude. Then he eased himself onto a corner of the desk. After Peacock told his part of the story, Luke told them about the bushwhacker who'd nearly killed him and the contents of the wire from Eastburn.

"It couldn't have been Gilmore who followed you and shot at you," said Fahl. "He was in plain sight at his saloon until all hours of the morning. It must have been Hatch, or maybe Lange."

"Or somebody they hired to do the job," said Isham.

"I don't think it was somebody they hired," said Luke. "The outlaws who work for them are holed up at one of the ranches Lange foreclosed on. It's too far away. There wouldn't have been time to ride out and recruit one."

"Maybe it was Hatch," said Isham.

"He could have been watching me," Luke agreed, "but the lights were on at his place of business and he was supposed to be working. He had Morgan and Dewitt to take care of."

"He might have left all that to his assistant, Barney Odem. He does that sometimes. With Hatch's addiction, Barney may be doing more than we know."

"Do you really think Mr. Hatch killed all of those women?" asked Lily with a shudder.

"According to Eastburn's wire he did."

"I doubt anyone would think Hatch is a choir boy," said Fahl. "What we've got here are four criminals who moved in and took over the city council. That ought to make Sinclair a headline that'll sell papers."

"Not yet," said Luke. "We want to catch them red-handed first."

Luke told them about how Lange and his partners had hired rustlers to steal cattle from a ranch until the rancher went under. Then the bank would foreclose and Lange would take over the place.

"Our local banker is building his own little empire," said Isham. "I wonder what the life expectancy of his partners might be."

"I'd guess about the same as Morgan's," said Luke. "What's more, they might just be smart enough to figure that out for themselves. Bledsoe has, at least."

He was interrupted by an insistent pounding on the door.

"Thunderation, Sinclair just don't quit when he smells a story," said Peacock.

Isham glanced out the window. "It's not Sinclair. It's Hatch's assistant, and he looks like he's about to have a fit."

Isham unbarred the door, and a ruddy-faced young man came rushing in. He gasped for breath.

"Just slow down, Barney," said Peacock. "What's got you in such an uproar?"

"It's the boss," he managed to gasp. "He's gone. It looks like he left in a hurry. His quarters are in the back, and I had a look to see if I could find him. His desk has been emptied. So has his chiffonier. All his bottles are gone too. You know the ones I'm talking about."

"Yeah," said Isham. "He took his laudanum supply."

"What am I going to do?"

"You've got them two ex-lawmen planted in the ground, haven't you?"

"Yes. But I've got another customer needing attention. Old Mr. Gaines passed away."

"Look, Barney," said Isham. "You've been working with Hatch for a long time, now. Don't you reckon you can do one of the customers solo?"

"I oft times do," said Odem. "Mr. Hatch isn't always able."

"Then you'll do just fine, Barney," said Lily, giving him an encouraging smile.

Luke had a thought. "Barney, was Hatch with you the night before last? I saw lights on at the funeral parlor."

Odem seemed surprised at the question. "As a matter of fact, he wasn't. Said he had important business to take care of and I was to carry on without him."

That substantiated what Luke had suspected. It had been Hatch who'd watched him leave town and had followed him. Hatch was the bushwhacker who'd come close to ending his life.

"Is that all, Marshal?" asked Odem. "I need to get on back."

"Yes, go ahead. You've been real helpful."

After the undertaker's assistant had gone, Luke turned to Russ Peacock. "It's probably best if you and Lily go on home. And be careful."

"I've got a business to run," said Lily. "We'll be all right at the café. No one would dare harm either of us there."

Luke recalled that Dewitt had drawn his pistol in the café, but he didn't think reminding her would serve any purpose.

"She's right about us having a business to run," said her father. "Don't worry, Marshal. We'll be fine."

"Go on then," said Luke. "And good luck with that news hound."

"Oh, I'll take care of Niles," Lily assured him. She put her arm around her father, and they left for the café.

"I've got business to take care of too," Luke told his deputies.

He followed the Peacocks out the door and headed for the funeral parlor. When he stepped inside, Odem seemed surprised to see him.

"Did you remember something, Marshal?" he inquired.

"I want to have a look at your boss' quarters."

"Of course. But he didn't leave anything of a personal nature behind. I already looked."

"If you don't mind, I'd like to see for myself."

Odem led him to the back of the establishment. Hatch's private rooms were a mess. He had one of those big French closets—an armoire, Luke thought it was called. It had been emptied. The drawers from Hatch's chiffonier had been pulled out. One lay on the floor. All were as empty as the armoire. The contents of his rolltop desk were gone as well.

After Hatch had missed his target he'd come back to Braxton and packed for a hasty getaway. Luke wondered how his partners would react to his defection. Rats always fled a sinking ship. Unfortunately, the remaining rats were dangerous.

Add Russ Peacock's unexpected appearance to the two defections, and Lange and Gilmore must be starting to make their own plans.

"Odem, where'd Hatch keep his horse?" he asked.

"Out in back. He's got a stable there. But he rents those black horses that pull the hearse from Sam Fletcher."

Luke stepped out to have a look. There were fresh horse droppings on the ground. Nearby was a set of tracks leading out of town. Hatch had made good his escape.

"Marshal, do you think Mr. Hatch is really mixed up in some of the bad stuff that's been going on around here?" inquired Odem, who had followed Luke and was hovering at his elbow.

"Looks like he was."

"Are you going after him?"

"I'm planning on it."

Odem's expression was downcast. "Looks like I'm going to lose my job."

Luke put his hand on the apprentice's shoulder. "Maybe

not," he said. "Maybe you can take the place over and run it yourself. You've learned all you need to know, haven't you?"

"I guess so," he said, as he considered taking such a big step. "Maybe I could."

Luke left Odem to mull over his options and headed for Coffer's place. He needed to exchange the dun for a fresh horse. Coffer was there and looking healthier than he had since the beating. He was eager for news about what had happened.

"Hatch grabbed his things and took off a little while ago. I just came from his establishment. I'm pretty sure that he was the bushwhacker who tried to kill me yesterday morning."

"Wouldn't put it past him," said Coffer. "It appears he missed."

"I can't take the credit. I let my guard down. It was the dun that warned me. It must have heard something, or else it was downwind and got a whiff of Hatch's horse."

"I'm floored at what happened to Russ," said Coffer. "He's lucky to be alive."

"He knows it."

"I never did think Bledsoe had the stomach to be a killer. Guess they had something powerful on him to get him to throw in with 'em."

"It was something like that," said Luke, keeping Bledsoe's troubles a secret.

"I'm going after Hatch." Luke went out back to the corral and whistled the blood bay over to the gate.

"You and I have some riding to do," he said to the gelding.

While Coffer watched and chatted, Luke switched his tack from the dun to the bay. Then he went out and filled his canteen with water from the pump.

"Here," said Coffer, who'd been to the back of the livery stable. He handed Luke a small gunnysack. "You're apt to get hungry."

Luke looked inside to find thick slices of light bread with cheese between them. There was also a turnip and a piece of smoked venison.

"Thanks, my friend. I appreciate this."

"Anytime," said Coffer. "You be careful now, Cochran. That Hatch is a desperate man, and he might not be quite right in the head after all that stuff he's been downing over the years."

He was referring to the laudanum. Remembering Eastburn's report about the murdered women, Luke resisted telling him that he didn't know the half of it. There was, indeed, something wrong in Hatch's head.

"If Peacock or one of my deputies drops by, tell them I went after Hatch. Otherwise I'd just as soon that word didn't get around."

The hostler nodded. "I know how to keep my mouth shut," he said.

The way Luke had it figured, Hatch didn't have much more than an hour's lead. His tracks were easy to follow. Once he was out in open country, Luke used his spyglass to try and spot his quarry. The terrain wasn't as level as it seemed, however. It was uneven, with dips and rises, making it impossible to spot the undertaker. He kept on his trail, following it like a bloodhound. It seemed clear that Hatch was headed for the Barton ranch to join the rustlers. If Luke failed to catch up with him before he got there, it would be one against many.

He thought about Hatch's attempt to kill him, and wondered if the bushwhacking was his own idea or if he'd drawn straws with Lange and Gilmore for the job.

When it came to partners, the number was diminishing. Morgan and Dewitt were dead. Bledsoe had been captured and defected.

Luke kept watch on his back trail in case either of them had seen him leave and had him followed. Next time he met up with Lange, he intended to arrest him no matter how many influential friends he claimed to have. He expected by that time the wanted dodgers with Moseman's picture would have arrived.

At length, Luke topped a rise and saw a rider in the distance. He was moving in a cloud of dust toward the Barton spread. He had no doubt it was Hatch. There was no way that Luke could catch him before he reached the outlaw haven. Still, he wanted to see the layout of the place and get an idea of how many were there. He dropped back, not wanting to tip Hatch off.

Autumn was well under way. The leaves of the cottonwoods that grew alongside a stream had turned a brilliant gold. To Luke's way of thinking, they were a prettier sight, by far, than any of those fabled golden cities.

It wouldn't be long before winter set in. He wanted to be back in Denver with Gareth for Christmas, wanted to see the little boy's eyes light up when his father gave him a sack of candy. But now he had a job to do. Now he had to keep alert and stay alive.

He spotted the house and outbuildings of the Barton

ranch when he topped another rise. The place spread out across a pretty valley. It was evident that the rancher who had owned it had invested a lot of work in his home. It was a shame to have lost it to a crooked banker with a bunch of rustlers in his employ. Quickly, he backed the bay down the slope to avoid being skylined. After taking a minute to hobble his mount, he made his way back to the top. There he lay, belly down, while he looked the place over with greater care.

Hatch was talking to one of the rustlers—no doubt their leader. Hatch was waving his hands around and acting more animated than Luke thought possible. It was clear they were having a disagreement. Finally, the two went inside the house. Luke counted four others that he could see. That meant at least five rustlers worked for Lange.

It occurred to him that if Lange had hired the out-laws, Hatch might not enjoy the same influence with them. Perhaps that was the cause of their argument. Luke wondered if the outlaw boss would send the undertaker packing.

He lay there for a long time, watching and waiting. The wind rustled the buffalo grass that grew all around him. A chipmunk bounded away when Luke made a sudden move to relieve a cramping muscle. Minutes ticked by. An hour must have passed before Hatch came out of the house and pulled the gear from his horse. It appeared that the outlaw had agreed to let him stay.

Luke crawled back down the slope and removed the hobbles from the bay. Then he mounted up and headed back toward Braxton. Hatch would wait. The crooked council member had no place else to go. It was time for Luke to turn his attention to Lange. He didn't think for one minute that Lange, or Moseman, would give up and trot off to a jail cell quietly.

Chapter Ten

Lange knelt on the polished pine floor in front of the safe. His heart beat fast as he filled a leather satchel and four saddlebags with cash. He'd put a CLOSED sign on the front door of the bank and sent the two tellers home so no one would walk in on him. He seethed with anger at having to do this, having to settle for what was in the safe, leaving the rest behind in its hiding place until later. At least he wasn't going to have to share with five others, not that he'd ever planned to cut them in. They were easily gotten rid of, like Morgan and his airheaded deputy. It had been an easy thing to shoot them through the bars.

With Bledsoe hiding out somewhere and Hatch on the run, things were coming apart. He had to salvage what he could and leave before Cochran got back to town. Under his breath, he cursed the marshal who'd been sent down from Denver. His plan had been going just fine until Cochran rode into town and started interfering. He still didn't know who sent for him. Maybe that trouble-maker Peacock had done it before he was shot. Although

it could have been Berry or McDougal just as well. Whoever had sent the message, the damage was done and it
couldn't be undone.

He finished filling the last saddlebag and began stuff-
ing the remaining bills into his pockets. When they were
full, he stuffed more into his boots. He was depositing
another handful in the crown of his hat when he heard the
back door squeak open. He froze. Someone had picked
the lock and was inside the bank. Lange was reaching
for the parlor gun that he kept inside the safe when the
click of a revolver stayed his hand.

"I wouldn't do that," said Gilmore in his slow-as-
molasses drawl.

Lange looked up to see the gambler standing in the
doorway. Gilmore was dapper as always, and he had a
pearl-inlaid Smith & Wesson revolver in his hand. Lange
jerked his hand away from the derringer as if it had suddenly turned into a rattler.

"Decide to take a trip to a healthier climate, did you?"
said Gilmore.

"What are you doing here?" Lange demanded, trying
to keep his voice steady. "You almost never leave the
Lucky Horseshoe."

"I make exceptions."

Lange was sweating, and his hands started to tremble. He hated for Gilmore to see him this way. His fear
was, no doubt, giving the cardsharp a lot of satisfaction.

"Look, Bledsoe's defected, and so has Hatch," he said
in an effort to justify his actions. "That marshal has made
a mess of my plans. There's nothing left to do but get out
while there's still time."

"I notice that you never mentioned anything about

your decision to me when we were having our little talk in my office, nor have you offered to give me my share of the profits. The way I see it, with the others gone, half of that money belongs to me now."

Lange was in trouble. He had to figure a way out, and quick.

"Sure, I realize that it's half yours," he said in a voice that he reserved for would-be depositors. "I was coming over to your place just as soon as I finished here."

"You take me for a fool?" said Gilmore. "You weren't planning to divide with anyone. Not even in the beginning. Now, where's the rest of the money? What you took from that safe is only a small part of what you've stolen."

"Of what *we've* stolen," Lange corrected him. "You needn't act so high and mighty. You were in on this too."

"Then there should be no dispute about my share. I want half, and I mean half, of all of it."

"And if I don't agree?"

"Then I'll take all of what you have right here, and I'll make sure you won't need the rest."

Lange swallowed hard and tried to keep control of his nerves. He'd made the mistake of underestimating Gilmore. He knew from the look in his partner's eyes that he meant business. Gilmore wouldn't hesitate to kill. In fact, if Lange were in Gilmore's place, he'd do the same thing.

"Get up from there," Gilmore ordered.

Lange staggered to his feet.

"Now you listen to me good, Moseman," he said, using Lange's real name. "The only thing that's keeping you alive is the fact that I happen to know you have a fortune hidden somewhere. Take me to it and I might let you live."

Sure you will. Lange had to think smart if he was to get out of this alive and keep the fortune that he'd stashed away. The gambler had surprised him. He'd always been the quiet, steady one. Hatch would have been more likely to pose a problem. At least he'd thought so until now.

"You don't dare shoot me here," he blustered. "The whole town will hear. They'll think you're robbing the bank."

Gilmore shot him a look of disgust. "Actually, I have another plan in mind."

He moved in quickly, before Lange realized what was happening, and hit him with the butt of the revolver. Lange crumpled to the floor.

Not wasting any time, Gilmore threw a blanket that he'd brought over Lange's prone body. Next, he carefully gathered all the money and restacked it inside the safe, including what was in Lange's hat, pocket, and boots. Then he shut the door. This accomplished, he picked up the empty saddlebags, along with the satchel, and stashed them in a corner of Lange's office. Finally, he dragged the banker outside and hefted him across the back of a horse. With an economy of movement, he tied the banker's hands. Then he ran the rope beneath the horse's belly and tied Lange's feet. The rope would keep him from sliding off. It would also prevent an escape. As an afterthought, he took the banker's keys from his pocket and locked the back door.

With the money returned to the safe, there would be no outcry about a bank robbery. When Lange was missed there would be speculation, of course. But the townspeople weren't apt to do anything more than gossip, at least for a long time. Cochran might be the lone exception.

With Lange's horse on a lead rope, Gilmore rode down to the end of the alley and headed out of town. After first checking his back trail, he turned and rode for a place he'd prepared for just such an occasion. It was a cabin in a remote canyon. There he would make Lange talk, for he had plenty of time. He'd left word at the saloon that he was going on a fishing trip and wouldn't be back for a while, so no one would be alarmed by his absence, not even Holly.

On the way, he thought about all the money Lange was holding out and what it could do for him. The Lucky Horseshoe was a paying proposition, but the money it brought in was not impressive. Braxton wasn't a big place, and there weren't all that many visitors. He wanted more to show for the years of living hand-to-mouth on riverboats and in frontier saloons. He wanted to go back to New Orleans with a new identity and plenty of money. There he would open a restaurant and gambling house for the rich and cultured. It would be a place with thick carpets on the floors and shining hardwoods. Crystal chandeliers would sparkle overhead. The servants would wear black suits and ties and have courtly manners. The name of his place would be famous throughout the South. He would, at last, be somebody. Just thinking about the future he had planned made him feel better. Making his dream a reality was worth what he'd had to endure from the likes of Lange and Hatch.

He was headed southwest, toward a canyon with no name. It was doubtful if any of the newcomers were aware of its existence. He'd learned of it from a drunken prospector who'd come into his saloon one night. The man's talk interested him, and he'd invited himself to his table. There, he'd treated the prospector to several drinks to further loosen his tongue. The fellow had told of the isolated canyon and its location. A short time later, Lange had gone looking for it, and he found the place just as it had been described. The abandoned cabin in the forgotten canyon made a perfect hideout.

He'd put a few more miles behind him when he heard a loud groan. His prisoner was coming around. It wasn't long before Lange started yelling.

"Let me loose! You can't do this to me!"

"So you finally decided to wake up," said Gilmore, experiencing a perverse pleasure in the arrogant man's predicament. "Have a nice nap?"

"Stop! I think I'm going to be sick."

While Gilmore didn't feel any sympathy for his former partner, he reined up and climbed down from the California sorrel that he'd bought in Santa Fe. He walked back and untied the rope that kept Lange fastened on the horse. As soon as the prisoner was free, he slid to the ground. With one hand, he reached up to feel the large knot that had risen on his head.

"Where are you taking me?" he demanded to know. "You'll never get away with this. My men will hunt you down and kill you."

Gilmore spit on the ground in disgust. "What men?" he said, his voice scathing. "Are you referring to those rustlers you've got holed up at the Barton ranch? Why, they don't know a thing about our little trip. What's more, I doubt they'd bother to help you if they did."

He could see that his words had hit Lange like a whip.

"What is it you're planning to do to me?" he asked in a quavering voice.

"I've got a place in mind where we can have a nice long talk. It's an isolated canyon that nobody knows about. When we get there I'll show you what happens to fellows who try to make off with all the money, fellows who kill their partners or else leave them behind to take the blame."

Lange sat on the ground looking up at him with something akin to terror in his eyes.

"Look, Mike, I wasn't going to cut you out, I swear. I was simply getting that money to a safe place where we could pick it up later and divide it like we agreed."

Gilmore stepped over and backhanded him. Lange reeled and went down on all fours. Blood trickled from the corner of his mouth.

"You insult my intelligence," said Gilmore. "I know exactly what you were doing. Now, when we arrive at our destination, you're going to tell me where you hid all the money you got from selling those ranches and the stolen cattle. And don't tell me it was all back there in that safe. I know better."

Lange eased back into a sitting position. "Listen to me, Mike," he said, his voice pleading. "I'm willing to make a deal. It'll be good for you, good for both of us."

Gilmore glared at him. "You're not in any position to make a deal. I'm going to ask you some questions when we get to the canyon, and I can promise that you're going to answer them truthfully."

Lange appeared to shrink into himself. He was in a bad fix, and he knew it.

"You're making a mistake," he whined. "We can still work together and make a fortune."

"We've already made a fortune, and I intend to have it. That's what this ride is all about."

Lange changed tactics and went from begging to threats. "Hatch is going to come after you, Gilmore. He's never liked you, and I wouldn't be surprised if Bledsoe doesn't join him."

"Dream all you want to," said Gilmore. "Now hold your hands out so I can bind your wrists. There's no sense tempting you to start trouble."

Lange pretended to obey. As soon as Gilmore leaned over, he slammed against him with all his weight, knocking him off balance. Before the gambler could recover, Lange kicked him hard in the mouth. He fell back, and Lange kicked him again. Then he grabbed the gun from Gilmore's belt and shot him in the chest. The gambler lay sprawled on the short grass plain, dead as he'd ever be.

"I always did admire this gun," Lange said of the pearl-handled Smith & Wesson. "I'm sure you won't mind if I take it along."

He searched Gilmore's saddlebags, but there was no money in them. Even the money he'd put in his pockets and slipped inside his boots was gone. He realized that Gilmore had put it back in the safe, not wanting a posse on his trail.

He climbed on the back of the gambler's California sorrel and took up the lead rope to his own horse.

"Sorry to leave you here without a proper burial, amigo, but I'm sure you understand that I don't have time for such niceties."

The way Lange saw it, he had no choice. He had to ride back to town and empty that safe again. Of course, he had another fortune hidden away, but he wasn't about to leave the assets of the Braxton Bank behind.

With Gilmore dead, he had one less problem to worry about. Bledsoe was a cowardly excuse for a man and Hatch was a weasel, but neither of them dared to say anything to the law about his projects. They had too much to lose.

His head ached, and it wasn't helped by a sun that was way too bright. He was certain he had a concussion. Still, he had to get back to town without being seen. Then he had to make a getaway.

Chapter Eleven

There was no longer any doubt. Stolen cattle were being held at the Barton ranch until they could be moved
out and sold. It was a perfect place to change the brands
and hold the cattle until the scars healed. It looked like
Hatch was going to hang around until he got his share
of the money. When his bushwhacking attempt failed,
he'd figured the jig was up in town.

Luke must have been halfway back to Braxton when
he spotted buzzards circling in the air. They were well
off the trail, but he was curious. What was drawing all
those scavengers?

"We'd better have a look, fella," he said to the bay, as
he reined up and pulled the spyglass from his pack. When
he put it to his eye he was surprised to see the body of a
man lying on the ground. He closed the spyglass sections
with a snap, wondering who the dead man could be. There
was only one way to find out.

When he drew near he could see it was Mike Gilmore. Somebody had shot the saloon owner at close

range and dead-on. Luke studied the signs that were left. Two horses and two men had come to this spot. The killer left with Gilmore's horse, which was rumored to be his pride and joy. One of those California sorrels, Isham had said. His fancy pearl-handled revolver was also missing.

There was more than one possibility for the murder. Someone who'd felt cheated at the Lucky Horseshoe might have brought him out here to get even. More likely, though, it was a falling-out among thieves. Gilmore was known to keep to himself when he wasn't working, so Luke doubted that he would have ridden this far from town without strong motivation. Since there was nothing he could do to help Gilmore—the gambler was beyond help—he left him there. When he got back to town, he'd send Barney Odem with a burial detail.

It was after dark when Luke rode into Braxton. There was a big commotion in front of the saloon. The lights were out in the Lucky Horseshoe, and the front doors were closed and locked tight. A group of thirsty would-be patrons had gathered in front and were hollering and pounding for the doors to open.

"Come down here and let us in!" yelled one of the protesters.

"You ain't got no right to shut us out!" yelled another.

There was no sign of either of Luke's deputies. No doubt they expected the noisy mob to give up and disperse. He figured that Braxton must be the only town in Colorado that didn't have at least two saloons, usually more. For sure, Gilmore had secured a monopoly on whiskey and gambling.

Luke rode up to them.

"Hey, Marshal, make Gilmore open the doors," said a man Luke remembered seeing around town a time or two.

"Sorry, I can't do that. Mike Gilmore was murdered today. Somebody shot him."

A ripple of murmured disbelief ran through the gathering.

"Can't the bartender open the doors?" asked a man who Luke recognized as the blacksmith.

No one appeared to be overly grieved about Gilmore himself. Their concern was with what he dispensed.

"It's not up to me," said Luke. "Why don't you boys all go on home. I expect somebody will open the place up tomorrow."

Grumbling, they dispersed and went their separate ways. Luke was left staring at the dark and deathly quiet saloon. Unfortunately, the Lucky Horseshoe hadn't been lucky for its owner.

The barkeep and the girls who waited on customers had either left the premises or else they were pretending they weren't there. They probably suspected something was wrong for, by all reports, Gilmore was rarely absent from his establishment. Luke had planned to break the news to someone inside, but those doors were apt to stay closed and locked, at least for now.

He rode on down the street to the bank. After dismounting, he went over and rattled the doorknob. The bank was locked up as tight as the saloon. Cautiously, he walked around to the back. That door was locked too.

He'd been told that Lange lived in an adobe house a block over from the main street. It was supposed to be the largest one in town, the kind of place you'd expect a rich banker to own. Luke found it in the moonlight. It, too, looked dark and deserted.

Luke slid out of the saddle and had a look around. The stable in back was empty, possibly a sign that Lange had left for good. The house was tightly shuttered, so there was no way that he could get a look inside without breaking in. It was his gut feeling that Gilmore and Lange had had a falling-out and Lange had shot him. But after that, what had the banker done? First thing in the morning, somebody needed to have a look inside the bank's safe. If Lange was anywhere around, Luke was going to arrest him.

Luke was bone tired and wanted nothing more than a good night's sleep. He headed over to the livery stable and found that Coffer was just getting ready to leave.

"Make yourself at home," said the hostler. "If you'll tell me what you've found out, I'll share this leftover slice of venison and the extra piece of pie that Lily sent over. I've got some coffee left too."

"You've got a deal," said Luke, finding a seat on a hay bale.

In between bites, he recounted what he'd seen at the Barton ranch.

"It's a shame that you couldn't have gone in there and arrested that no-account Hatch and hauled him back here," said Coffer. "But with five or more of them outlaws ready to shoot on sight, you'd never have got the job done."

"That's kinda the way I had it figured too. He'll stay there, though. You can bet on it. Hatch needs money and the protection of them rustlers. You can ride in there next week and I'd wager he'll still be there."

Luke told him then about finding Gilmore's body.

"Who'd have thought? It couldn't have been Hatch, and you've got Bledsoe stashed away. It had to be Lange who done it."

"That's how I had it figured," said Luke. "It appears that Lange has fled."

"Wonder where he went."

That was a good question. Luke had been giving it a lot of thought.

"Gilmore was a man who kept to himself as much as he could," said Coffer. "Oh, he'd make appearances in the saloon every night, and he seemed to be right fond of that girl named Holly, but he usually preferred his own company."

"Did he have any enemies, aside from his partners in crime?"

"None that I know of. With Gilmore's high-tone ways and all, the young women around here seemed to think he was something special. On the rare occasions he left the saloon, it would cause a stir. A bunch of 'em would be trying to catch a glimpse of him. One or two of the bolder ones would walk right up to him and try to pass the time of day. He was always a gentleman, of course, but he sure didn't encourage none of 'em."

To Luke's way of thinking, Mike Gilmore was a strange and complicated man.

"I doubt if anyone would call Hobart Lange a gentleman," he said. "From what I hear, he walked roughshod over a lot of people. I'd say he has a real knack for making enemies."

"More'n any of the rest of 'em, unless you count Morgan and Dewitt. Hatch always walked around dosing out fake sympathy for the bereaved relatives who needed his services. He wasn't easy to warm up to, but he wasn't strongly disliked. As for Bledsoe, folks around here actually liked the fellow, once they got past his fuss-budget ways."

"Both Hatch and Bledsoe are out of the way for now."

"How come you don't arrest Lange and lock him up?"

"I intend to—just as soon as I can find him."

Coffer got up and took Luke's empty plate and coffee cup. "I'll be leaving you to get some rest now," he said. "You know, Marshal, you're always welcome here."

"I appreciate that, my friend."

After Coffer had gone, Luke rubbed down the gelding and fastened on a feed bag of oats. Then he spread his blankets in the loft. Tired as he was, it didn't take him long to fall asleep. It was dawn when he awoke. He climbed down the ladder and went out to the pump, where he threw a few handfuls of water at his face, washing the remnants of sleep away. Then he ran his fingers across the stubble on his chin but decided against shaving. There was no time. Quickly, he gathered his bedding and made a roll of it.

"It's your turn today," he told the lineback dun before throwing a saddle over its back.

In spite of the fact that he looked downright scruffy, he decided to stop at the café before he went looking for Lange. He wanted to tell the Peacocks what he believed had happened between Lange and Gilmore. He was leading the dun out of the livery stable into the early morning light when he felt a blow that brought him to his knees. The blow was accompanied by a loud report. Startled, the dun shied away. Luke put his hand to his side. It came away covered in warm blood. Keeping low, he drew his pistol. He tried to spot the sniper, but he was nowhere to be seen. Someone was shouting. He could hear the sound of running feet. There was another shot. His head jerked and felt like it was about to explode. Then a black curtain descended.

Luke struggled to open his eyes. The inside of his mouth felt like it was lined with cotton. There was a dull pain in his head and another in his side. He could tell he was lying in a real bed. When he opened his eyes, he saw yellow curtains at the window. He tried to sit up and moaned from the effort. Lily Peacock appeared in the doorway. She was a vision dressed in blue and smelling of flowers.

"Thank heaven you're awake at last," she said as she moved to his bedside.

He struggled to remember how he came to be in this strange bedroom.

"What happened?" he asked with difficulty, his mouth so dry he could scarcely form words.

"You were shot when you left the livery stable. The bullet missed the vital organs, but you bled a lot. Another bullet grazed your head."

"Please, some water."

"Of course. Just a moment."

She hurried out and returned a short time later with a glass of water in hand.

"Sip slowly," she warned as she gave it to him. "You don't want to make yourself sick."

Luke doubted if he could make himself feel any sicker than he already did.

The water tasted good as it moistened the inside of his mouth and slipped down his parched throat. He sipped slowly until he'd finished the whole glass. All the while, a thousand questions were churning in his mind.

"Did anyone see who shot me?"

She took the glass from him and nodded.

"Jamie Dodd saw Hobart Lange clearly, and his mother caught a quick glimpse of Lange as he was riding away. There isn't any doubt. Lange was laying in wait for you behind the corner of the feed and grain store next door. Deputy Isham found a couple of spent shells where he'd been standing."

"I take it Lange rode out of town."

"Faster than a cat with its tail on fire. What's more, he took the contents of the bank safe with him."

No surprise there.

"How long have I been like this?"

She placed her hand on his forehead as if checking to see if he was running a fever.

"Luke, you were shot three days ago," she said softly. "My father and I have been taking care of you. You're in our home."

He'd lost three days of his life. It was hard to believe.

"Did anyone go after Lange?"

"Yes. Deputy Isham trailed him for a time, but the wind came up and wiped out the tracks. He expected Lange to ride for the Barton ranch, but he veered off. He thinks that Lange didn't want to lead a posse to the stolen cattle and doesn't realize that you all know of his hide-out."

"Could be," he said, though he doubted that was the reason.

Lily looked concerned. "Try to rest now," she said. "I'll leave you alone."

After she'd gone, he lay there, mulling the situation over. If he were in Lange's place, he wouldn't be hauling all that loot out to the Barton ranch where it would tempt the money-hungry rustlers. He'd have another place to go, one that was known only to him.

Luke made an effort to get out of bed but failed. Getting back on his feet was going to take a little time.

Two more days passed before he was able to get up and get dressed, an attempt that was supervised by Russ Peacock. Luke experienced only a little dizziness, but he was still weak.

"We had to get rid of your old clothes," said Peacock. "They were a mess."

The ones he was wearing were new and freshly laundered.

"I'm obliged for all you and your daughter have done for me," he said, feeling that words were inadequate.

"You saved my life coming after me the way you did, Marshal. Besides, you're a good man and a good friend."

"You appear to be feeling better," said Lily when he made an appearance in the kitchen. "Are you hungry?"

"I'm as hungry as a bear after six months in hibernation," he said.

"Good. But I expect you'd better start out with chicken soup. Chicken soup is good for everything."

"If you'll excuse me," said Peacock, "I've got to get back to the café."

After he left, Luke felt a pang of guilt for causing the father and daughter so much trouble.

"Here," said Lily, setting a steaming bowl of soup in front of him.

To his way of thinking, nothing ever tasted so good. He ate two bowls of it.

When he'd finished, he felt a lot better. He decided it was time to broach the subject of his weapons.

"I'm going to need my guns and my horse," he said.

Lily looked surprised. "Mr. Coffer has them over at the livery stable. But surely you're not planning to go after Lange so soon after being wounded."

"The trail is already five days cold. I don't want it to get any colder."

"Then for heaven's sake, don't go alone. You can scarcely sit on a horse."

"Don't worry about me," he said. "I'll be fine. And thanks again for all that you and your father have done. I'm in your debt."

"Quite the reverse is true," said Lily. "After all, you brought my father home. Now, please take another day or two to recuperate."

"Maybe I will," he said. "But I'm going over to have a talk with Coffer. I want to clean my guns and have everything ready to go when I'm able to ride."

Lily smiled. "Mr. Coffer predicted you'd say that. He's one jump ahead of you. He cleaned your guns the day you were shot. Said he knew you pretty well, and that you were too stubborn to stay abed long."

Luke felt a strong sense of friendship toward Coffer, the Peacocks, Ham Isham, and a few others like he'd never felt for anyone up in Denver. If it was within his power, he was going to track down Lange and get their money back. Lange, or Moseman, was going to keep a date with the hangman.

Chapter Twelve

Iț's good to see you up and around, Marshal," said Coffer when Luke walked into the livery stable on legs that were still a little shaky.

"Glad to be here," said Luke. "Guess I'm going to have to be a lot more careful from now on."

Coffer laid aside the harness he was mending and motioned Luke to a seat.

"There've been a lot of complaints since Gilmore's murder," he said. "The Lucky Horseshoe has been locked up tighter than a drum since the day he left town. Isham and a couple of others went out and buried him. But nobody's taken charge of the saloon and opened it."

"Did Gilmore have any relatives who might inherit the place?"

"None that anybody knows about, but there's a rumor going around that he left a will. The lawyer who was supposed to have drawn it up for him has his office over at Parsons. Guess we'll find out in good time."

Luke looked up to see Isham standing in the doorway with a grin on his face. "Good morning," he said. "Miss Lily told me I'd find you here. You're sure looking a lot better than the last time I saw you."

"I expect so," he said wryly.

"I saw you heading over here. I don't guess you're going to be well enough to lead a posse."

"To the contrary, I'm well enough to ride," said Luke. "But a posse isn't needed."

Isham looked surprised. "Why do you say that?"

Luke explained his reasoning. "We know that Lange didn't go to the Barton place. He's a man who doesn't like to share, even with his partners. If those rustlers were to discover the stolen money that he's carrying, they'd take it away from him. Lange's headed for someplace else, a place that he's prepared ahead of time. The fact that his tracks veered off supports that theory. We don't need a posse. One man, or two, will be plenty."

"What about Gilmore?" said Coffer. "Do you suppose that's where Lange was taking him before they had their falling-out?"

"Probably," said Luke, "or maybe Gilmore was taking Lange, and Lange turned the tables on him."

Isham mulled that over. "It sounds reasonable," he said. "We could try to find the spot again where Lange's tracks left the trail."

Luke began strapping on the .44 that Coffer had cleaned for him.

"When I found Gilmore's body," he said, "it was a considerable distance off the trail. If it hadn't been for those vultures, I wouldn't have known to go and look. I think that's where I should start tracking Lange."

"You mean that's where the two of us should start," Isham amended. "I'm going with you."

Luke had learned to depend on the man. There was no one he'd rather have at his side as he tracked down a vicious killer.

"Fine," he said. "We'll pull out in the morning at first light. Be ready to ride."

No sooner had Isham taken his leave than Lily came rushing in. It took her a moment to catch her breath.

"What's the matter?" he asked.

"You have to come back to the house with me," she said. "There's someone waiting to see you."

He wondered what visitor could have sent Lily scurrying like this to fetch him.

"I'll come with you," he said, "but at my own pace. Whoever it is can wait a few extra minutes."

"Of course, Luke," she said, using his first name. "I know you can't go trotting around wounded the way you are. Still, I promise you won't want to keep this person waiting overlong."

"Who is it?" he asked, his curiosity piqued.

"You'll find out when you get there. I can't say anything more."

Coffer raised an eyebrow. "Oh, don't mind me," he said. "I didn't hear a thing. But you'd better go with her, Marshal, else she's apt to get upset."

Luke escorted Lily back to her house at a more leisurely pace. They were greeted on the way with a "Good to see you up and around, Marshal" and "We've been praying for you, Marshal." It gave him a sense of satisfaction to know he was accepted by the towns-people.

When he walked into the kitchen he was surprised to find the saloon girl sitting there. She was the one whom he'd talked to when he'd gone to see Gilmore. What was it they called her? Holly? She was dressed in conserva-tive clothes and had her hair pulled back and fastened in a neat bun. Looking at her, no one would guess where she earned her living. Holly had what his sister-in-law would call class.

"Marshal, I have to talk to you," she said. "It's about Mike."

"If you'll excuse me, I have some wash to hang on the line," said Lily, tactfully leaving them alone.

Luke pulled out another chair and sat across the table from Holly.

"I've come to see you, Marshal, because I want you to catch Mike's killer."

She was twisting a handkerchief in her hands and was close to tears.

"Ma'am, I'd like to do that, and I'll try my best."

"There's something you should know that might help," she said. "I think that it was Mike who was taking Lange to a hiding place that he knew about. He didn't trust Lange. He was doing things that Mike didn't approve of. I think that somehow Lange got the upper hand and killed Mike. Before he died, I think Mike must have told him about that hideout, and I'd bet a great deal that he's there now."

What she said made a lot of sense when he thought about the death scene he'd come upon. It would also explain how Lange had seemingly disappeared off the face of the earth with all that money.

"I've heard things about Hobart Lange," said Holly. "Sometimes, after a few drinks, Mike would talk. Lange gets into trouble, lays low for a while, and then reinvents himself. He changes his name, disguises his looks, and creates a made-up past to fool people."

Luke already knew that he'd done this at least once.

"Have you got any idea where Gilmore's hideout might be?" he asked.

"Maybe. Mike got a little drunk one time and was talking about a canyon with no name, a canyon that no one knew about. He said the mouth was narrow and brush covered, and it was way off from any trail. It would be easy to pass it by unless you were looking for it. Mike was told about it by an old prospector who'd come into the saloon to cadge some free drinks."

This canyon sounded like the perfect place for a bank-robbing killer to lie low for a while.

"Thanks for the information, Holly," he said. "I'll go look for this canyon with no name. Maybe I'll find it, and maybe I'll find Lange."

"Are you really able to ride, Marshal?"

"I was already planning on heading out in the morning with Isham."

She looked at him like she wasn't betting he could make it to the privy by himself, let alone ride for no telling how many miles over rough country.

"You're a good man, Marshal," she said, standing as if preparing to leave. "I'll thank you when you catch Mike's killer. By the way, there's been such a clamor for the saloon to open that Dave, the bartender, is going to open the doors. They can work out who owns it later."

"Guess that'll make some of the folks around here happy," he said as he escorted her to the door.

She left then, leaving behind the scent of lilacs. It was the same perfume she'd been wearing the first time he'd met her. Lily appeared about a minute and a half later.

"Was her information helpful?" she asked.

"Maybe." He told her about Gilmore's canyon with no name.

"So you and Deputy Isham intend to ride out in the morning all by yourselves? Shouldn't you take along more men? If you do happen to find Lange, you'll be in serious trouble."

"I don't want to tip him off. Just the two of us might be able to sneak up on him."

Lily pushed back a wisp of hair that had escaped from her hairpins. She looked worried.

"You need to recover that money he took from the bank," she said. "A lot of it belongs to the people around here, and they can't afford to lose it."

"I'll do my best," he promised.

That night he slept in the loft of the livery stable once more. It was a big change from the soft bed at the Peacocks' house, but somehow he felt more at home here. At dawn he was ready to ride. Isham met him outside right on time.

"You sure you want to do this?" said his deputy.

"I'm sure."

"Then Homer can take care of the town while we're gone. If he needs help, he can call on Coffer and some of the others."

With all the outlaws somewhere else, Luke doubted Fahl would have any trouble or need any help. He turned the bay's nose toward the sunrise and, once again, rode out of town.

Dawn was his favorite time of day. He liked watching the sun's colors inch their way above the edge of the horizon. Chipmunks and prairie dogs, squirrels and birds on the wing were awake and busy with the work of finding food. Even the air smelled fresher in the early morning. His narrow escape from death had made him more aware of everything around him. It also made him yearn for his son. When this was over, he was going straight back to Denver and spending time with Gareth. Eastburn could send someone else to the far corners of the Territory for a change.

He and Isham stayed on the trail until they had to veer off to reach the spot where Gilmore had been shot.

"I've got a feeling that you know something I don't," said Isham as Luke searched the area for signs of Lange's direction.

"Maybe. Do you know that girl Holly who works at the saloon?"

"I've seen her," he said. "She's a right pretty young woman. I heard tell that Gilmore was besotted with her."

"She told me that Gilmore got drunk one night and started rambling on about a secret canyon that an old prospector had told him about. Holly suspects that Gilmore was going there with Lange when Lange shot him. She thinks our fugitive might be holed up in that canyon with his stolen loot."

"So did she tell you where it is?"

"She didn't know. But I'm starting here, where I found Gilmore's body. This is a considerable distance off the trail between Braxton and the Barton ranch. I figure Gilmore was heading toward the southwest. As I recall, there's some rough country down that way. A small canyon might well be hidden there."

"Well, if Gilmore and that prospector were the only ones who knew about it, the place must be harder to find than a whiskey bottle at a camp meeting. We're going to need some luck."

Luke agreed. Trouble was, when you weren't expecting it, Lady Luck was apt to show up and ask you for a dance. But when you really needed her, she was likely to be hiding out on the moon.

"This way," said Luke, and the two lawmen continued to ride in a southwesterly direction.

Six days had passed, days when the wind had blown. There was almost no trail left to follow. Still, Luke kept on because he had a strong hunch that he was on the right track. After a time, he reined up.

"You're not giving up, are you?" asked Isham, at his side.

"No. But the trail is cold. We're on our own. Still, I don't think the canyon we're looking for would be much farther away from town than this. Gilmore wouldn't be interested in a place that was so distant it would keep him from his duties at the Lucky Horseshoe overlong."

"Then what do we do now?"

"Let's swing due south a ways and then double back across different country. It may be that we bypassed it to the north."

"Guess that's about all we can do," Isham agreed, wiping his brow with a red bandanna. In spite of the fall day, the sun was hot.

Luke took a swig from his canteen. The wound in his side still pained him, and the long ride hadn't helped. On top of that, he felt weak. It was a gamble as to whether or not his strength would hold out.

"You're not looking so good, partner," said Isham, who was eyeing him closely. "I think we'd better stop for a while. I brought some provisions along. You look like you could use something to eat."

He was right. Besides, Luke didn't feel like arguing.

They walked the horses to the shade of a piñon. There, Isham built a small fire and put on a pot of coffee to boil. After they'd eaten a meal of fried bacon and cold biscuits and washed it down with the hot brew, Luke felt a little better.

"Get some rest," said Isham. "I'll keep watch."

Knowing that he'd need all the strength he could muster if and when he encountered Lange, Luke spread out his blankets and went to sleep. A couple of hours passed before Isham nudged him awake.

"We'd best get a move on if you want to make a sweep of the land farther south. It'll be dark before you know it."

Rest and food had worked wonders. Luke felt almost human again. He rolled up his blankets and fastened them behind the cantle of the bay. Then he mounted up and led the way south. Isham followed on his grullo, a big slate blue horse with a dark mane.

Their journey had taken them into an isolated area that was rougher and more arid. As they rode farther south, the landscape became wilder and more broken. Luke could see how it would be easy to hide a canyon in the midst of all this.

Another hour passed before he decided to turn back to the east. The going was slower now. There was no way to rush without risking injury to the horses. Luke didn't know how long the uneasy feeling had been creeping up on him, but it finally reached the point where it couldn't be ignored.

"Careful, Isham," he said. "I think somebody is following us."

He rode behind the cover of a large rock and motioned his deputy to follow. Once out of sight, Luke reached for his spyglass. He climbed down from the saddle and crept around the rock that hid them. Keeping low, and shading the lens of the spyglass so that it wouldn't reflect any sunlight, he scanned the terrain over which they'd come. It took only a few seconds to spot the man who was trailing them.

"I see him," he said.

"Anybody we know?"

"Yeah. It's Charlie from the McDougal ranch. Now, what's that old fellow up to, I wonder?"

"Don't reckon we'll have to wait long to find out."

When Charlie drew near, Luke stepped out of hiding and called to him.

"What in blazes are you doing so far from home?" Luke asked.

"I've been trailing you fellows ever since Coffer, at the livery stable, told me you was off to find Lange. He said there was only two of you, and I figured you could use some help."

His help wasn't something Luke wanted, but now he had no choice. Charlie was a good man who meant well.

"Glad to have you along," Luke said, as if he really meant it.

They were quite the threesome to go up against a vicious killer like Lange. A wounded marshal, a cow nurse, and a man old enough to be Luke's grandfather. Luke sure hoped Lady Luck was hanging out close by.

Chapter Thirteen

Lange had waited until after dark to revisit the bank and his house. He was thankful that his nocturnal arrival had failed to attract any notice. All the citizens who weren't in their homes were gathered in front of the Lucky Horseshoe, which hadn't opened its doors. He wondered if the saloon would ever open again. If it did, it would be under new management.

He rode Gilmore's sorrel and led his own horse down the alley to the bank. There he unlocked the back door. After a quick glance around to make sure no one was watching, he slipped inside. Feeling his way in the dark, he retrieved the satchel and saddlebags that had been thrown into a corner of his office. Then he shut the door and lit a small lamp. By its light, he filled the containers once again with the contents of the safe. When this was done, he snuffed the lamp and loaded a fortune on the backs of the horses.

Next, he stopped at his house and picked up the few belongings he was loath to leave behind, including his

Missouri mule. He took time to switch the load his horse was carrying to the mule. Then, mounting the sorrel again, he led the two animals over to the livery stable.

There was a light on in the jail, but neither of Cochran's horses was tied out front. He figured Coffer would know the marshal's whereabouts.

Outside the livery barn he paused when he heard voices. He wrapped the lead rope around his saddle horn. Then, keeping the reins of the sorrel in his hand, he climbed down.

Under the cover of darkness, he moved in closer and listened. Cochran was back and, curse the luck, he'd discovered Gilmore's body. What's more, he knew who'd done the killing and wasn't going to stop until he had the killer in jail.

Lange's heart pounded so hard that he was afraid it would burst out of his chest. He'd almost left town without knowing there would be a bulldog like the marshal hot on his trail. No two ways about it, Cochran had to die.

Quietly, he led the horses and mule away from the livery stable and around to the other side of the feed and grain store next door. There, in the darkest of shadows, he'd wait. It would be a long night, but he couldn't leave without killing the man who was determined to destroy him. If he knew Cochran, he'd be riding out at first light. It would be the last light he'd ever see.

Lange was hidden and waiting when he saw the marshal head out of the livery stable. The distance wasn't far. He raised his pistol and fired. Cochran went down. Lange fired again. Then he kicked the sorrel in its sides and made a run for it.

He was counting on confusion and disorganization to allow him to escape. Without Cochran, there was no clear leader. This had bought him some time. Hopefully, it had bought him lots of it.

By nightfall he was ensconced in the cabin hideout, the one Gilmore had believed to be his alone. Sitting in the doorway, looking up at the stars, he cursed the bad luck that had turned his plans sour. That bad luck had come down from Denver wearing a badge and carrying a pistol. But things had changed. Luke Cochran was dead. What's more, Lange still had the money he'd stashed away, as well as the money he'd taken from the bank. All together, he'd have enough to make a prosperous new start somewhere else.

As for Gilmore and Hatch, he'd been planning to get rid of them in his own good time. Bledsoe too. Gilmore had simply hurried things along in that regard. Lange's head still hurt where Gilmore had pistol-whipped him, so he didn't regret the gambler's death one whit.

He didn't like it that Hatch and Bledsoe were still on the loose. No doubt they still expected a share of his money. He had every right to think of it as his money. Hadn't he been the brains behind the operation? Hadn't he taken most of the risks? Well, the others weren't going to get a single greenback of it.

Gilmore had been so smug about his secret canyon that he thought no one else knew about. How wrong he'd been. Lange had known about it all along. He'd been hoping to learn of a rich mining claim, so he'd taken that old prospector home and plied him with his housekeeper's good cooking. He'd popped the cork on a fine bottle of wine as well, a wine that demanded seconds and thirds, a wine that loosened lips. That old man, Doyle was his name, didn't say anything about gold, but he talked about his secret canyon in great detail. Gilmore hadn't realized that he was a Johnny-come-lately.

Now there was nothing to do but rest awhile and maybe read a book that he'd brought along. After a time, things would die down in Braxton. So would the fervor to send out a posse. Then he would leave his hideout and travel on, making sure to avoid the Barton ranch. He figured that was where Hatch had gone. Let him cool his heels there until the rustlers got tired of waiting for a new job. He didn't know where Bledsoe was, and he'd stopped caring. Whatever the spineless creature babbled about would amount to nothing, for Hobart Lange would soon cease to exist.

Who would he be next? He needed a name that was dignified and important sounding, one that would command respect. He thought of the presidents. Jefferson sounded dignified. Jefferson had been a member of the Virginia Tidewater aristocracy. His mother had been a Randolph, no less. That would make a fine moniker. Adams would be too obvious a last name to go with it, though, and Madison didn't sound right. Pierce did, however, although from what he'd read, Franklin Pierce hadn't amounted to much. He tried the name out—Jefferson Pierce. He liked the sound of it.

He dared not go east no matter how effective his new identity. He was too well-known, and disguises could be seen through by anyone who was intent on looking. California might be a place where he could settle in. With all the money he'd managed to accumulate, San Francisco might provide a pleasant respite.

Lange went to bed that night feeling better than he'd felt in a long time. The following days were almost idyllic.

When darkness caught up with Luke and his companions, they stopped and made camp. The terrain they were in was far too rough to risk night-riding. Isham built a small campfire where it couldn't be seen from a distance, and they warmed themselves with hot coffee and more of Isham's fried bacon and biscuits. Charlie fished a can of peaches from his saddlebag and opened it with a knife. To Luke, the meal seemed like a feast. He was feeling the effects of the long ride, but food and coffee always helped. Charlie looked tired too.

"Charlie, what made you leave your nice soft bed and Louisa's good cooking?" he said, half jokingly.

McDougal's cousin had stretched out and was resting his head against his saddle, which he'd placed on the ground.

"Well, you see, it's like this," he replied. "I'm tired of being the old man who's sitting in his rocker watching everybody else do important things. I want to be out doing things myself."

"I'd be the first to admit that hunting down Lange is important," said Isham, "but you were helping to guard Bledsoe. That's important too."

"That fellow doesn't need guarding. He's safer with McDougal than anyplace else, and he knows it. Besides, I don't think he's got it in him to kill a grasshopper, even if it got in his way. I believe him when he says them charges against him back in Kansas was trumped up and the real killer helped him to escape."

Isham muttered an agreement.

"Anyway," he went on, "when I got to town and heard what had happened, I took out after you. I figured to help you round up that sidewinder Lange."

"Don't get me wrong, we welcome your help," said Isham, "but you may wish you'd stayed away before this is over."

Luke silently agreed. He was too tired to reason with the old man, though. He was too tired to do anything except drift off to sleep.

When he opened his eyes, there was just enough light to see by. He got up and looked around. Nothing seemed amiss. He listened for the sounds of nature, but everything was quiet at this early-morning hour save for the whisper of wind through the piñons. Charlie crawled out of his blankets and looked down at the sleeping Isham.

"Do you reckon we should leave him to catch up on his beauty sleep?" the old man asked.

"Might as well," said Luke.

"I heard that," said Isham, rolling out of his bed. "I was playing possum."

"No time for play," said Charlie. "We'd best get a move on."

After a quick meal, they mounted up and headed out.

"This is a big country," said Charlie. "Mind if I ask how you expect to find that canyon when you don't know where to look?"

A good question, thought Luke. The information he was relying on was skimpy at best.

"From what Holly at the Lucky Horseshoe told me, I suspect that Gilmore was killed while he was taking Lange to this hiding place. I found his remains a considerable distance off the trail. It appeared that he was headed this way. You've got to admit that the rough country around here could easily hide a canyon."

"Still, that's not much to go on," said Charlie.

"I think Gilmore must have visited that canyon earlier in order to check it out. It wouldn't have been so far from town that the trip would have taken him away from the Lucky Horseshoe for long. He didn't strike me as the type who'd be comfortable leaving his profitable business in the hands of his employees."

"But what makes you think he was there before?" said Isham, squinting into the distance as if he were trying to pick out the canyon from everything else.

"I'm wondering about that too," said Charlie.

"Think about it," said Luke. "I believe that in the beginning of that jaunt, Gilmore was the one in charge. He rode out of Braxton with a man who'd become his enemy. It has to follow that he was confident of finding the canyon straightaway. Otherwise, he'd have been in trouble. The only way he could be confident was to have checked out the canyon's location and its suitability ahead of time."

"Makes sense to me," said Isham. "Now, if we could just find it."

"Wish he'd given that girl Holly a map to the place," said Charlie. "It'd sure make our job a lot easier."

Luke's job was rarely easy. The three of them continued on in silence for a long stretch. It had been fully daylight for some time now, and only a few fluffy clouds dotted the bright blue canopy of sky. He kept alert for any sign of an entrance to the hidden canyon.

They were moving ever eastward now, and he was beginning to doubt his reasoning. But if he were wrong, where else could Lange have gone? Isham had contacted the railroad authorities as soon as Luke was shot. There had been no sign of him at the depots in the area, nor had anyone been caught stealing a ride. If he'd gone to Parsons, Pete Brosseau would have spotted him and sent word. Lange was too smart to go to the Barton ranch, and he dared not go to any of the others.

They were climbing higher. He could tell by the changing plants and shrubs around them. He scanned the horizon. Overhead, in the distance, a hawk searched for prey. Luke watched as the winged hunter swooped low. Strangely, it disappeared from sight as if plunging into an arroyo—or a canyon.

"Did you see that?" he asked his companions.

"Looks like that might be the place we're looking for up ahead," said Isham.

Single file, they picked their way over the rough ground. At last they found what they'd been looking for. Half hidden in rocks and scrub was the entrance to a canyon.

"You think this could be the right one?" said Isham in a hushed tone.

"From Holly's secondhand description, I'd bet on it," said Luke.

"If Lange is in there, he's well armed," warned Charlie. "He might be watching the entrance."

"I doubt it," said Luke. "Remember, he thinks he's in a safe place that no one knows exists. Even if he was worried about being tracked, he'd expect anyone from Braxton to approach from the other way. We've come the long way around."

"That happens sometimes when you don't know where you're going," said Isham. "It's a wonder we found this place at all."

Again they rode single file as they entered the canyon. Junipers and scrubby piñon pines covered the slopes. Sound echoed in canyons, so Luke and the others made as little noise as possible. Gilmore had it right, as far as Luke was concerned. This was an ideal hiding place. It was only because of the gambler's drunken conversation with a barmaid, and her desire for justice, that Luke had known to come looking.

As they rode deeper into the unnamed canyon, the sloping walls rose higher. Here, tall pines covered the slopes and spread over much of the canyon floor. Luke was surrounded by their pungent perfume. He listened as the wind rustled through their needled branches. The canyon floor had widened, and he could hear a stream burbling over rocks somewhere off to the side.

They were far from where they'd entered when a sudden flash of movement caught Luke's eye. His hand went to his gun, but he eased it back when he saw the outline of a doe bounding up the slope.

"Appears to be lots of game in here, along with fresh water," said Charlie softly. "It's a regular Garden of Eden."

This was true, thought Luke, but like the original garden, there was a serpent lurking somewhere within.

A little farther along, he spotted a plume of smoke. It appeared to be rising from a chimney. Luke reined up and signaled the others to stop.

"He's up there," he said, pointing to a cabin that was almost completely hidden among the trees and scrub.

"Good thing you spotted that," said Isham. "He can sit up there and pick off anyone who approaches from either direction."

"You reckon he's seen us yet?" said Charlie, shading his eyes with his hand to see more clearly.

"He hasn't started shooting," said Luke. "I expect that's a good sign."

"Maybe we'd better fan out," said Isham. "Like this, we make easy targets for a man with a rifle."

"I've got an idea," said Luke. "I'm going to ease my way up that slope and circle around to the back of the cabin. The two of you leave the horses and get as close as you can to the front of the place without being seen. Whenever the shooting starts, I'm counting on you to back me up."

"Good thinking, Marshal," said Charlie. "I've got to admit this beats that front porch rocking chair and then some."

Luke dismounted and grabbed a rifle from his saddle boot. After wrapping the reins around a branch, he started the long climb. He kept low, hoping that Lange wouldn't spot him. Charlie could complain all he wanted, but compared to what Luke was about to do, a front porch rocker would look real good.

Chapter Fourteen

Lange had managed to make himself halfway comfortable in the abandoned cabin. It contained a few pieces of rough-hewn furniture and a workable fireplace. The supplies he'd hastily gathered from his house would last for a time. Besides, there were the things that he'd brought the first time he'd come here. After his supplies ran out, he could hunt—or leave. He preferred to leave, but not prematurely. With Cochran dead, he felt more secure. Still, the marshal at Denver could send another deputy to Braxton. He might even send more because Cochran had been shot. But that would take time, and his trail was already cold.

No doubt the bank depositors would be clamoring to get their money back, for all the good it would do them. Isham and Fahl were all they had in the way of law officers now. He didn't think Fahl could find his way out of a gunnysack, and he doubted Isham would strike out on his own and raise a posse. On a cold trail like his, a posse, no matter how fired up, would do no good.

Lange dragged a stool outside and sat beneath the overhang of the cabin. Pulling one of his cigars from his pocket, he cut the end with his knife and lit it. There was something pleasurable about the aroma of a good cigar, he thought. Once he was away from this place, he would begin to live a more genteel life. Maybe he'd marry if he happened to find the right woman, one who wasn't snoopy. Possibly he'd revive his interest in politics, though not in a visible way where nosy reporters were apt to ask questions and investigate his past. Rather, he would find his place behind the scenes. Understanding human nature as he did, he knew it wouldn't be hard to get something on a politician, something the man didn't want the public to know. Once he did, he owned that fellow. Whatever power the politician wielded would become his power. The thought was even more pleasurable than the cigar.

It was a shame that he couldn't have gotten something on Cochran. That way, he could have stayed on in Braxton. He could have taken over the surrounding area and lived like a tsar. Even buying the marshal off would have been worth the cost. But he had Cochran sized up as a man who wouldn't tarnish his precious badge by accepting a bribe. And what had that badge gotten him? A small salary, countless days in the saddle, and an early grave. Some men never learned.

As he sat there, thinking about his future, he got an uneasy feeling. He tried to shrug it off, but it only got stronger. He squinted and looked across the canyon. Suddenly, he caught a glimpse of something in the distance. Something was moving along the canyon floor. He didn't have a clear view. It could have been a deer.

Then, too, it could have been a horse. He kicked over the stool in his hurry to get inside.

When he first arrived at the canyon, Lange had buried one of the saddlebags and the satchel in a shallow hole he dug beyond the stable, but he'd kept the other saddlebag with him. Not wasting any time, he fastened his gun belt around his waist and tossed the nearby saddlebag across his shoulder. Next, he grabbed his rifle. He might be jumping at shadows, but with all that was at stake, he couldn't afford to take any chances.

He took another look out the front. This time he saw a horse, plain as day. He caught a glimpse of its rider as well. Still as a statue, he watched. There were two more. It puzzled him that they were coming from an unexpected direction. But even if it wasn't a posse from Braxton, their presence here spelled trouble.

He had to act fast. After making sure that he had plenty of ammunition, he slipped out the back way and headed for the stable. The sorrel whinnied as if it sensed another horse besides its stablemate nearby. There was an answering call from down in the canyon.

Wasting no time, he saddled up. The forest was his best chance. Hidden among the trees, he would have the freedom to maneuver and possibly get the drop on his enemies. The dull green shirt and brown pants that he was wearing would blend into the landscape. He was thankful he'd had the foresight to buy them.

Keeping low, Luke inched his way up the slope. If Lange was worried at all about being trailed, he would likely be focusing on the other direction. At least that's what he hoped. Still, he remembered Eastburn's oft re-

peated admonition: *Never underestimate the enemy.*
Another was *Never make assumptions.* He hoped that
Charlie and Isham were staying out of sight.

To his dismay, he heard a horse whinny from the
cabin's stable. *Don't answer,* Luke silently willed the
three horses that had brought them here. It was no use.
A faint answer echoed from below. If Lange was paying
attention, he would have heard. The element of surprise
had been lost.

There was no turning back now. Trusting that the other
two were hidden below, Luke continued to make his
way up the slope. Suddenly a flash of lightning rent the
sky. Thunder echoed through the canyon. He had been
caught off guard. Distracted by the task of hunting his
quarry, he hadn't noticed the bank of clouds that had
rapidly moved in.

It had been raining in the mountains. If that rainwater
rushed downward and was channeled through arroyos, it
would rush through the canyon. The horses were in dan-
ger. He looked down to where they'd been tied and saw
Charlie on his way back for them. The old man would
lead them to higher ground. Isham remained hidden.
Luke could barely make him out through the branches.
He trusted his deputy to know when to make his move.

The sky opened up then and started dumping bucket-
fuls of water. Luke shielded his rifle beneath his duster,
which also covered his pistol. Rain dripped from his hat
and obscured his vision. It didn't take long for the rain-
saturated soil to turn into a slippery slide. He dug in his
heels to keep from losing ground and struggled on.

When he reached the cabin, it appeared to be deserted.
But there was an overturned stool at the front door, and

the smell of coffee emanated from inside. Lange had been there a short time ago. Pistol drawn, Luke rushed through the doorway. The place was empty, just as he'd thought. Lange had spotted them and gone out the back way.

Suspecting a possible ambush, Luke went out the front and circled around the side of the cabin until he had a clear view of the stable. The gully washer had erased the killer's footprints. Partly shielded by the corner of the cabin, he scanned the area for any sign of where the outlaw was lurking. Without warning, a lightning bolt struck a tree only a few yards away. The noise caused a disturbance in the stable. There were horses inside. But was Lange in there too?

After taking a deep breath, he ran a zigzag path toward the ramshackle affair. He'd gone no more than a dozen steps when his foot slipped in the mud and he went down on all fours. An instant before he hit the ground, he heard a gunshot. Lange had fired at him. No doubt the fall had saved his life. It was clear that the outlaw wasn't holed up in the stable. From the sound of it, he was somewhere on the slope above, hidden among the trees.

Luke crawled backward until he found cover behind a cluster of snowberry bushes.

"Get out of here!" yelled Lange. "Go back to where you came from!"

Luke didn't answer. No sense letting the outlaw know exactly where to target his shots.

After the single shot and Lange's outburst, there was quiet. Except for the pounding rain and an occasional clap of thunder, there was no other sound. Charlie and

Isham were laying low. The wind had risen. Luke, clad in rain-soaked clothes, was chilled to the bone. He clamped his jaw shut to keep his teeth from chattering. The way he saw it, he had to either draw Lange out of his hiding place or else go up there after him. He got to his knees and brought up his rifle, which he'd managed to keep out of the mud.

"Lange!" he called. "Give yourself up. You're not going to get away."

"I thought you were dead, Cochran. I tried my best, you know."

Fueled by anger, Luke squeezed off a shot and then lunged to the side. Lange returned fire, and white berries from the snowberry bushes flew in every direction. Luke scampered to the protection of a young pine. As he hunkered down behind its thick branches, he heard Lange laughing. It was a maniacal laugh with no humor in it. He tried to spot the outlaw, but Lange was taking care to stay out of sight.

Luke drew a deep breath and settled back to wait. Lange's laughter faded, and then there was silence. The sudden cloudburst eased off, leaving the slopes muddy and hard to climb. Still, the warming sun was a relief.

Luke wondered if he should signal for Isham and Charlie. Maybe the three of them could surround Lange and disarm him. Before he could whistle for them, Lange yelled to get his attention.

"Look, Cochran," he said, "do you really expect me to turn all my hard-earned money over to you and ride back to Braxton as docile as a sheep? You know I wouldn't stand a chance."

"You'd get a fair trial," said Luke, looking in the

direction of Lange's voice and trying to make him out. "I can promise you that."

Lange scoffed at his reassurance. "Oh, I'm sure I would. And after that fair trial, you'd all come out to the necktie party. No thank you. I'm staying put. Come after me if you dare."

"Tell me something, Lange. Why'd you kill Gilmore? After all, he was your partner."

"Oh, sure he was. When I was emptying the bank's safe, he picked the lock and came in. Then he pistol-whipped me and put the money back. When I woke up, he was on his way to this place. He thought this was his secret hideout. I got loose and shot him. The man got greedy, that's all. He didn't want the people's money that I was taking from the bank. He wanted the money I had stashed away. He thought rustling money and the profits from selling foreclosed ranches wasn't as dirty as the bank money. He was going to bring me here and make me tell him where I'd stashed it."

Lange's story was pretty close to what Luke had already guessed.

"What Gilmore didn't know," Lange continued, "was that I knew about this canyon before he did. Gilmore wasn't near as smart as he thought he was."

Luke was hoping that Lange wasn't either.

Suddenly, he heard Lange's horse moving away. He didn't think the outlaw would go far, though. Not while he had a fortune hidden someplace nearby.

A thick carpet of pine needles had been laid down over time and, slick with rain, they were as hazardous as the mud. There was no way that Charlie and Isham would be able to climb the slope quickly. Until they could reach him, Luke was on his own.

Maybe this was the way it was supposed to be, one against one. After all, he was Eastburn's best deputy, and he was the one who had the Marshal's badge pinned on.

Keeping low, he left the cover of the pine, and going from tree to tree, he made it to the stable. From this new vantage point, he scanned the area for a glimpse of the shooter, but there was no sign of him. He decided to try an old trick. He took his rifle and put his hat on the end of the barrel. Then he exposed the hat by moving it out about a foot from the wall of the stable. The response was immediate. Two quick shots tore through the stillness. One made a hole through the crown of his hat. Lange had revealed his location. Bringing his rifle to bear, Luke fired off a couple of rounds of his own. There was no sound after that. He didn't know if Lange had been hit or if he was dead. Luke wasn't counting on either one. He wasn't making any assumptions.

"Marshal!" came a shout from below. "Are you hurt?"

It was Isham.

"I'm fine!"

He slipped inside the stable and looked around where the rain hadn't washed out any tracks. A horse and a mule were stabled there. The horse that Lange was riding had been there. The outlaw was free to maneuver and, with a fortune at stake, it was a sure thing that he would try to pick them off.

Luke stepped outside the stable and fanned an arc of gunfire as quickly as he could squeeze the trigger. Then, keeping his head low, he sprinted toward the trees where he believed Lange was hiding. He'd almost made it when Lange started shooting. Luke felt a bullet slam into his side, very near his previous wound. Then his knees buckled and he went down.

There were more gunshots, this time coming from below. His partners were drawing Lange's fire away from him.

Luke struggled to pick up the rifle that had slipped from his hands. He felt faint.

"I've got it," said Isham, who'd made it up the slope. "We've got to get you inside."

Charlie was firing into the trees, keeping the outlaw busy.

Isham handed Luke the fallen rifle before pulling him to his feet. Then, putting Luke's arm across his shoulder, he staggered toward the stable with his burden. It was then that one of Lange's bullets found its mark. Isham went down, dragging Luke with him. Now they were both sitting ducks. Charlie alone was holding Lange off.

Luke pushed Isham aside so he could help Charlie. Pain jabbed through him like a knife. This was the second time Lange had drawn his blood in a week. Luke was mad. He staggered to his feet and plunged forward, trusting Charlie to keep the outlaw's attention. He managed to make it to the edge of the woods.

Close as he was, he could see Lange clearly now. The outlaw had mounted Gilmore's big sorrel. Luke drew his pistol and called out, "Give it up, Lange. It's all over."

The outlaw let go with a curse and spurred the horse directly toward Luke. Luke was forced to lunge aside to keep from being run down. Before he could turn and get a shot at Lange, the outlaw was out of sight, shielded by the branches of the pines. Luke stumbled to his feet. He'd already lost a lot of blood. Now he was losing more. The bleeding had to stop. When he staggered to the edge of the trees, he saw Charlie kneeling beside Isham's body.

"Is he . . ." Luke asked, knowing the answer already.

Charlie nodded. "It looks like he took a bullet right in the heart. The poor fellow didn't stand a chance."

Luke swore. "I'm going to get that lowlife killer if it's the last thing I do."

"Well, Marshal, if'n you don't get that hole plugged up that he put in you, you're not going to live long enough," said Charlie. "I've got some stuff. Let me fix you up."

Charlie helped him down to the cabin. Then he went and fetched his supplies and some dry clothes from their saddlebags. Deftly, he cleaned and bandaged Luke's wound.

"Better get some dry clothes on, Marshal," he said. "I brought the horses up to the stable. I'll take care of 'em later."

While the old man started a fire in the fireplace, Luke stripped off his wet things and got into dry ones, warming himself at the fire until his teeth stopped chattering.

"What about Isham?" he said.

Charlie shook his head and looked mournful.

"He was a good man. I'll get him buried. You're not in any shape to."

"Lange got away again."

"It appears so."

Luke hadn't felt so defeated since his wife's death. He

tried to think like the outlaw. Where would Lange go, now? What would he do?

"I sure am going to hate to tell Deputy Fahl about his friend," said Charlie.

"I know what you mean. Ham Isham was a good man and a good friend."

Luke eased himself closer to the fire.

"I heard one time what his real name was," said Charlie. "It's Alexander Hamilton Isham. Now that's a moniker to make a fellow sit up and take notice."

Luke agreed. Now, however, it was simply a name to be carved on a headstone.

Charlie took pieces of venison jerky from his supplies, added some other ingredients, and made hot soup. Luke ate it gratefully.

"Now you get some sleep," said Charlie. "I'll keep watch in case that owlhoot decides to double back and surprise us."

Luke didn't need urging. He was exhausted. His body had taken a beating over the past half-dozen days, and he needed to rest and recover. Just as he was falling asleep, he thought of the money. What Lange had stolen from the bank was only a raindrop in the bucket compared to what he'd gotten from the rustled cattle and foreclosed ranches. Luke would bet a month's salary that the loot was hidden right here in this canyon. Very likely, it was hidden near the cabin. The trick was to find it without getting killed.

Chapter Fifteen

When Luke opened his eyes it was dark as pitch. His freshly wounded side throbbed, and his mouth felt dry. He lay there quietly, trying to recall the details of what had happened. What it came down to was that Lange had gotten away and Isham was dead. He pushed himself into a sitting position.

"Feeling any better?" said Charlie from a dark corner of the cabin.

"Some," he said. "Hear anything moving out there?"

"Nope. But I figure Lange knows where we are. There's not been a peep out of the horses, though. Guess nothing's been out there bothering them."

"Why don't you try and get some sleep, my friend?" Luke said. "I'll keep watch until daylight."

"If you're feeling up to it, I could use a little shut-eye. I expect tomorrow is apt to be a long day."

He was right, and Luke hoped they would both live through it.

Charlie leaned his rifle against the wall and bedded down. Before long, his rhythmic breathing turned into snoring. Luke had been annoyed when the old man had insisted on tagging along, but now he was glad to have him. Charlie had wanted to do important things. Well, he was doing them.

Luke found his canteen and took a drink, letting the cold water slip down his parched throat. Then he nudged the door open and slipped outside into the night. There was a chill in the air now that the sun was no longer warming the canyon. He took a deep breath and filled his lungs. It served to wake up his senses.

When the storm moved on to the east it had left everything in the canyon smelling fresh and clean. The sky was clear, and the stars were as bright as he'd ever seen them. He'd had another close call. How many times could he rely on luck to save him from these attempts on his life? He thought again of Isham. Come morning they'd have to bury him.

He glanced up at the Big Dipper. By its placement as it rotated around the North Star he reckoned there was a good three hours left before sunrise. They needed to be ready. There wasn't a doubt in his mind that Lange would double back to retrieve the fortune he'd amassed.

While he stood there looking over the night-shrouded canyon, his thoughts turned to his son. He would like to make a home for him in a small town like Braxton, at least a Braxton that was clean of corruption. He'd like to be able to spend each day with him, or at least some portion of it. Life was too short for these long separations, and Gareth was growing fast. Luke was missing so much that could never be retrieved. This would be his last assignment, he decided. It was time for a change.

He stood there a while longer, listening to the wind whisper through the pines. It was a wind song that swept over a canyon of death.

Shortly before dawn, Luke and Charlie ate the rest of the venison soup.

"Guess we'd better get to it," said the old man when they'd finished. "One of us has got to keep watch while the other does the work."

"We'll switch off," said Luke.

"The way you've been shot up, I'm not sure you're able to be scratching out a hole for a grave. Not in this hard soil."

Luke wasn't sure either, but for Isham he was willing to give it a try.

"I've got me one of them little fold-up shovels in my pack," said Charlie, "but I don't know how long it will last in this rocky ground. I'll make the grave shallow and cover it with rocks."

Luke stood guard with his rifle while Charlie went to work. He scanned the forest that surrounded them for any sign of movement. Lange wasn't going to sneak up on them if he had anything to say about it.

Charlie insisted on doing all the work himself, and after the burial he piled rocks on top. When the chore was done, he pulled the bandana from around his neck and wiped the sweat of exertion from his face.

"Want to say any words over him, Marshal?" he asked. "I think Ham would like it if you did."

The request took him by surprise. Luke wasn't much

of a speaker, and he couldn't recall any Scriptures off-hand that he could recite.

"I'll just say that Ham Isham was a good man and a fine deputy. The world could use more like him."

"Amen to that," said Charlie fervently. "It sure could."

Lange spent a cold, wet night wrapped in his blankets on a bed of pine needles. Had he taken better aim, Cochran would be dead and Lange would be dry and comfortable in the cabin that he considered to be his own. It wasn't simply a matter of getting away with the money now. He had a score to settle. He was going to make Cochran wish he'd never left Denver. It pleased him to know that he'd put lead into that nosy marshal yet again and that Isham was either dead or so badly wounded that he wouldn't ever amount to anything. All Cochran had left to help him was that old geezer who lived out at the McDougal place. No doubt they'd be tracking him come daylight. That is, if Cochran was able to ride. Let them come. He'd be waiting for them.

At dawn he was urging the sorrel up the slope to where a boulder perched precariously on a narrow shelf. He'd noticed it on his first trip to the canyon. Leaving his horse nearby, he approached the huge rock. After putting on his pince-nez glasses, he examined it closely. It appeared that with a little leverage, he could pry the boulder loose and send it rolling down the side of the canyon where it would crush anyone in its path. If he could lure his enemies to the right spot, he had a powerful weapon.

First, though, he'd wait for them to come for him. Chances were good that he could pick them off from behind cover. Cochran was obviously a good tracker, so finding Lange's trail and following it would be an easy task. Lange fetched his mount and tethered it behind a large pine. Then he settled down behind some scrub to wait. He was wrapped in a dry blanket, but that was the extent of his creature comforts. All of his supplies had been left behind in the cabin. He longed for the warmth of a hot cup of coffee, not to mention a decent meal. Cochran and that crazy old man were going to pay for this.

The sun was far above the horizon by the time they'd buried Isham. Luke would have been worried about the head start Lange had gotten, except he was certain the outlaw wouldn't leave the canyon without the money he'd stolen.

"Where do you reckon he stashed all that loot?" said Charlie, looking back toward the cabin.

"Somewhere close by, I expect."

"He must have buried it."

"It's likely."

"Well, if you're not in a big hurry," said Charlie, "why don't we have us a look around? Maybe we can spot something."

"You go ahead and have a look. I've got a chore to do before we leave."

While Charlie wandered around outside the cabin, Luke went to the stable where he fed and watered the horse and mule that Lange had left behind. He took care of the other three horses as well. When he'd finished and was leaving, something caught his eye. A few paces from the southeast corner of the stable the dirt had a different look about it. It had been smoothed flat, much flatter than the surrounding rocky area.

It was the way a place would look if it had been dug up and then the hole had been covered again.

"Charlie!" he called. "Come here and bring that shovel of yours. I need it."

"You find something?" said Charlie, as he came trotting around the corner of the cabin, shovel in hand.

"Maybe. Maybe not. We'll soon find out."

"If you want, I'll do the digging while you keep a lookout."

"Let me start. If I have to stop, you can take over."

Thankfully the rain had softened the soil here, and it came away without much effort. It took only a few shovelfuls to uncover what was hidden. Charlie leaned over and retrieved a leather satchel and a pair of saddlebags. They were all stuffed with money.

"I don't know if this is all the loot that was taken from the bank," he said, "but it's a whole lot of it."

Luke felt a sense of satisfaction knowing what this money meant to the people who had trusted the bank.

"I'll wager that this isn't all that Lange has stashed around here," he said. "Somewhere, there are all the profits he made from stealing cattle and ranches."

Charlie looked at him with a puzzled expression on his face. "You got any idea where to look, Marshal?"

That was the problem. He didn't. "No. Still, I'm guessing that it's been buried around here someplace, just like this stash was."

"We'd best go after Lange then, since he's the only one who can tell us where to look."

That's what Luke intended to do, just as soon as he got all the stolen money loaded onto Isham's horse. He didn't hold out much hope that Lange would reveal the whereabouts of his ill-gotten gains, however. The outlaw wasn't apt to surrender. Since he knew what was lurking in his future, he'd likely fight to the death.

Charlie must have been thinking the same thing. "If he's not able to tell us where it's hid," he said, "I doubt that money will ever be recovered."

While it would be a shame to lose the money, Luke figured that stopping a killer like Lange was more important.

Before they left the cabin, Charlie made Luke hold still while he pulled the old bandages off and doused both his new wound and his old one with alcohol. Then he applied fresh bandages.

"You're almost as good as Doc Vanhelden," Luke said. "Thanks."

"I've done a lot of doctoring in my time. Wish I had some of that laudanum Hatch was so fond of hoarding, though. It'd ease the hurt."

Luke wished he had some too, for all the good it did him.

"I'll go saddle the horses," said Charlie. "I'll bring Isham's along on a lead rope and let Lange's horse and mule run loose. Wouldn't want 'em to starve if nobody is able to come back for 'em."

Luke nodded. There was no way of knowing if anyone would survive the confrontation that was sure to come.

They headed for the nearby trees where they'd last seen Lange. Single file, they made their way among them. Luke picked up Lange's trail easily, and he and Charlie followed it. From the broken limbs and disturbed pine needles, it was clear which way he'd gone. They kept silent, listening for the enemy.

Luke wound his way through stately pines and Gambel oaks. Charlie followed close behind. After a time, the trees began to thin out.

"Looks like there's a clearing up ahead," said Luke softly. "If I were Lange, I'd be waiting to ambush us when we entered that open space. There'd be no cover at all."

"I see what you're saying," said Charlie. "It's ready-made for an ambush."

"You wait here," said Luke. He dismounted and handed Charlie the reins.

"I'm going to the edge to have a look around."

Quietly, he made his way forward to the very edge of a large clearing. He scanned the area for any sign of movement. When he looked up the slope, he noticed that a large boulder was perched precariously on a narrow ledge. From the looks of it, a few more heavy rainfalls would erode its underpinnings enough to send it tumbling to the canyon floor. He wondered if Lange might have noticed this too. One thing was for sure, when that ledge gave way, that big rock would crush everything in its path. With a little help it could be launched prematurely.

A shiver ran down his spine, as if somebody was walking over his grave. He had to admit that this was the way Lange thought, and Lange knew they'd be tracking him. He figured the chances were good that the outlaw was up there, waiting for them to ride into the clearing. If Lange didn't get them with his rifle, he'd crush them under a ton of stone.

Silently Luke eased farther back into the forest and returned to where Charlie was waiting.

"I'd bet a month's salary that Lange is up there waiting for us," he said softly. "There's a boulder about to give way. I think he intends to help it."

"What have you got in mind, Marshal?"

"Stay under cover, but get Lange's attention. Shoot toward that boulder. Move around a little so he'll think we're both down here. While you're keeping him busy, I'm going to circle around and climb up there. I'll try to get behind him."

"I've got Isham's rifle too, so I can shoot off a lot of rounds without having to reload."

"Good. Keep him occupied."

On foot, Luke headed up the slope beneath the cover of the trees. Below, Charlie started shooting. At first there was no response. Then Lange started shooting back. Luke's hunch had been right.

As he closed in on the outlaw, the air around him was thick with gun smoke.

When he drew level with the boulder, he continued climbing until he was above it and looking down on the sniper. Lange was focused on Charlie. But just as Luke was getting ready to leap onto the outlaw and take him prisoner, a stone rolled beneath his foot and he tripped. Alerted by the sound, Lange turned. Tossing the rifle to his other hand, the outlaw drew his pistol. But the smoke was dense, and he fired at a level that would kill a standing man. Luke, however, was down in the dirt, desperately trying to get his footing.

Lange yelled a curse at him. A sudden gust of wind cleared the smoke enough for the outlaw to see him clearly. Luke rolled to his left an instant before a second shot was fired. Spurred by desperation, he managed to get his feet under him. Before Lange could fire again, he lunged.

The two grappled as Luke tried to wrest Lange's pistol away from him. Then Lange hit him in his wounded side. Luke doubled over in agony and went to his knees. When he looked up, Lange had an ivory-inlaid pistol aimed right at him. His face was twisted with hatred.

"I've been itching to put a bullet into you ever since you first walked into my office at the bank that day," he said.

"You've put a couple of 'em into me already," Luke replied, holding the man's gaze as he scooped a handful of dirt.

"Third time's the charm," said Lange.

Before the outlaw could squeeze off a shot, Luke slung the handful of dirt into his eyes and dived out of his line of fire. Knowing he had only a second or two, he grabbed his pistol and fired off two quick shots. The wind had cleared the air enough for Luke to see blood forming a blossom on the front of the outlaw's shirt.

"I can't believe . . . ," Lange started as he slipped into a sitting position.

"Want to tell me where you hid all that money you made from rustling and stealing ranches? You're not going to be able to use it now."

"Find it yourself," said Lange. They were his last words.

"You all right up there, Marshal?" Charlie called from below.

"I'm fine. Lange is dead. Come on up and help me search him and his belongings. Maybe we can find a clue as to where he hid the rest of the loot."

The search revealed nothing except the rest of the money from the bank. It was like they were on a treasure hunt with no map and no clues.

"You don't even know for sure that it's here in the canyon," said Charlie.

"True. But it seems a reasonable guess."

"You going to bury Lange?"

"Nope. I'm taking him back to Braxton. I think a lot of people are going to want assurance that he's dead."

The two of them managed to wrap the body in a ground cloth and fasten it across the back of the sorrel. Then they went back to the cabin to round up the horse and mule they had turned loose. Neither had wandered far from the stable.

"I'm going to have a quick look around the outside of the cabin," said Luke. "Maybe the earth has been disturbed where he buried that money."

"I'll get the animals ready to leave and be waiting for you," said Charlie, who'd lost interest in hunting for a treasure that would be next to impossible to find. He was satisfied with having recovered the bank money.

Luke tried to put himself in the outlaw's place. As a banker, Lange was accustomed to secure vaults and safes. While he might bury a satchel of money in the dirt in an emergency, he'd want something more substantial for the greater part of his fortune. If Luke's theory was correct, this would eliminate everything but the cabin. The money had to be somewhere inside.

He stepped through the doorway and looked around. The floor was dirt. The roof was held up by beams and provided no hiding place. The only possibility was the fireplace. It was built of large stones gathered from the canyon. He walked over and began checking to see if any were loose. It didn't take long to find one. A large stone at the far end of the hearth slipped out, as did two others beside it. They revealed a deep cavity, one that was filled with stacks of greenbacks. Each stack had a waterproof covering and was tied with a string.

"I've found it!" he shouted.

Charlie appeared in the doorway. "Well I'll be . . . ," he exclaimed. "You sure as sin did."

"Give me a hand here."

Charlie produced some gunnysacks from his seemingly endless store, and they loaded the money into the sacks. When they were securely fastened onto Lange's mule and his spare horse, Luke and Charlie started down the slope.

"I've got a feeling that an awful lot of people are going to be relieved to see us," said Charlie.

Luke knew he was referring to the return of the bank's stolen loot, but he didn't like to be carrying the news of Isham's death. He was especially dreading to tell Homer Fahl and Lyman Berry. The one consolation was the fact that Lange's killing days were over.

"What are we going to do about Hatch and that nest of rustlers up at the Barton place?" Charlie wondered aloud as they neared the mouth of the canyon.

"I'll go after 'em, I guess," said Luke. "It happens to be my job."

What he really wanted was a good meal, some relief from the pain in his side, and a good night's sleep in a real bed.

Chapter Sixteen

It was well past nightfall by the time they got back to Braxton. When they rode into town, the main street was deserted. The only signs of life were at the Lucky Horseshoe, where light and sound flowed out from beneath the swinging doors. The barkeep had opened the saloon, and the patrons had returned. Luke figured everyone else was at home. He envied men who had families to go home to after a day's work.

He and Charlie reined up in front of the jailhouse hitching rail. A lamp had been lit inside. But Fahl startled him when he stepped out of the shadows.

"Keeping an eye on the town?" Luke said to the deputy, painfully dismounting from his weary horse.

"I figured it would be a good idea," said Fahl, "since I didn't have anybody to do it for me. I'm glad you finally decided to show up."

Fahl's attention was suddenly drawn to the sorrel's burden.

"What have you got there?"

"It's Lange," said Charlie. "What's left of him anyway. We brought him back, along with all the loot he stole."

"That's good news," said Fahl, glancing down the street as if looking for a third rider. "Where's Ham?" he asked.

This was the time Luke had been dreading.

"I'm afraid we've got some bad news, as well as good," he said. "Isham took a bullet. He's dead. We buried him on the slope of the canyon where he was shot. I'm sorry. He was a good man."

Fahl didn't say anything for a minute. It appeared that he was trying to get a grip on the idea that his friend was gone for good.

"Did you bury him proper, with words and every-thing?" he said at last, his voice husky with emotion.

"We sure did," Charlie piped up before Luke could say anything about the brief and simple proceedings.

"Berry's not going to like hearing that he was killed," said Fahl. "Him and Ham were longtime friends too."

Luke already had that figured. He hoped he wasn't going to be the one to tell him.

"Come on inside," said Fahl. "It's too dark to bury Lange tonight. We can do it in the morning just as well."

The way Luke was feeling, he didn't care if Lange ever got buried.

Once inside, the deputy noticed that Luke had been wounded again.

"Looks like you're hurt, Marshal," he said.

"I still haven't learned to duck when the lead starts flying."

Luke remembered the money then. "If you two wouldn't

mind unloading those bags, I think it'd be a good idea to lock them in the jail for tonight."

"You've got a point there," said Charlie.

When the burlap bags of money were safely stashed in one of the cells and the door was locked, Fahl brought Luke a laudanum bottle.

"This is what the stuff was meant to be used for," he said as he handed it over. "Take a dose now and when you need it."

Luke did as he was told. It wasn't long before the pain had eased and he began feeling drowsy.

"Why don't you go back to one of the cells and try to get some sleep," said Charlie. "You're all wore out. I'll take the horses over to the livery stable and see that they're took care of."

Luke didn't argue, for he could barely keep his eyes open. He'd have to wait and get something to eat in the morning before he rode out after Hatch. When he lay down on one of the cots, he immediately fell asleep.

The next morning, when he went to the café with Charlie to have breakfast, both Peacocks were on the job.

"We heard you brought in Lange last night," said Lily, who was looking almost as happy as when she'd been reunited with her father. "That couldn't have been easy."

"No, it cost Isham his life," said Luke.

Lily gasped and seemed speechless for once. Evidently they hadn't heard that part of the story.

"Ham Isham was a good man," said Peacock. "Did you bring him in too?"

"No. We buried him on the slope of the canyon, not far from where he died. It seemed like the right thing to do."

"You could have done worse," Peacock agreed. "Guess you know that Barney Odem has taken over Hatch's business. I expect he'll be burying Lange today."

"We learned something else," said Lily. "Mike Gilmore left the Lucky Horseshoe to Holly Bradford. She's going to be running it. I'm really happy for her."

Luke figured Holly was the only one who had any good feelings for the gambler, and she deserved her inheritance.

Before Luke and Charlie could finish their eggs and biscuits, Niles Sinclair came hurrying in, pad and pencil in hand.

"What's the story, Marshal?" he said. "This is great news for the *Braxton Bugle*."

Sinclair could be pesky, but Luke liked him in spite of it.

"The story's not over," he said. "I'm raising a posse to go after Hatch and the rustlers that he's holed up with."

"Count me in," said Peacock. "I know Fahl will want to ride along too."

"As will I," said Sinclair.

"There's going to be shooting," said Charlie. "You and that pad of paper are apt to get in the way. Might even get shot at. It's best you stay here and let us bring the news back to you."

Sinclair frowned. "Are you telling me to stay back here in town too, Marshal?"

After the past couple of days, Luke didn't feel like getting into an argument with a green-behind-the-ears reporter.

"If you're bound and determined to go," he said, "then come along. Just don't get in the way. And when the shooting starts, you'd better run for cover."

Sinclair looked as happy as a kid with a bagful of candy at Christmas.

After breakfast, Luke rounded up his posse. When it was done, there was Coffer, Odem, Gil Clay from the feed and grain store, Russ Peacock, Charlie, Fahl, and Sinclair. That made seven men who were willing to ride with him, although he was skeptical about how much help Sinclair and Odem would be.

Doc Vanhelden came to the jail and cleaned his wound again before applying a fresh bandage.

"This makes twice that you were lucky," said the doctor. "I guess it wouldn't do any good to tell you to get a room at the hotel and take it easy for a few days."

"I'd like nothing better," he said, "but I can't. Not right now, anyway."

"I know. You've still got work to do. Well, be careful."

Luke's posse was waiting for him outside. This was the last part of his assignment. As far as he was concerned, Bledsoe was welcome to come back to town and live and work here the rest of his life. From what he could tell, the townspeople felt the same way, since the storekeeper wasn't a killer and had simply been blackmailed by Lange.

Luke stepped into the dun's saddle. His .44 had been cleaned and so had his rifle. It was time to ride.

The sun was in the west and slipping lower when they topped the rise that gave them a clear view of the Barton ranch. They were skylined, and one of the outlaws spotted them. He raised the alarm. The other four came running and saw the posse that was poised to descend on them. There would be no element of surprise.

"Hold still," Luke ordered. "Let them get the full effect."

While the eight of them lined the top of the hill, showing the outlaws their strength in numbers, a couple of the rustlers trotted for the corral.

"Hey," said Sinclair, "it looks like two of them are making a run for it."

"Let 'em go," said Luke. "It'll make things tougher for the three that's left."

The two who'd decided to leave didn't waste any time getting saddles on their horses and mounting up. They were heading out when one of the other rustlers spotted them. Without warning, the rustler turned and fired two shots at their backs. Both riders fell. Neither had seen death coming.

"Did you see that?" said Sinclair, astonished at what had just occurred. "That fellow went and shot his own men in the back."

"It's the price they had to pay for running out on their partners, I guess," said Peacock.

"I'd like to know where Hatch is hiding out at," said Charlie. "I don't see him anywhere."

Luke had been wondering about the undertaker himself. Maybe he'd been so scared that he'd left the ranch without waiting for his share of the money. That didn't seem likely, though.

"Are we going to ride down there now?" said Fahl, impatient to get started.

"Yes, it's time," said Luke. "Have your rifles ready. When we get within range, pick your target and fire. They'll be shooting at us. I'm going to circle around and try to get behind them. Maybe get them to surrender."

While Luke and his posse rode down the hill, the three remaining outlaws took cover. It wasn't going to be easy to take them, but Luke had never expected it would be.

It was one of the outlaws who fired the first shot. It didn't come anywhere close, but it started the ball. The air was soon filled with gun smoke. Luke used the cover to take off and circle around the entrenched outlaws. The posse was doing a good job of keeping the rustlers' attention riveted on them. Before the shooting had started he'd seen that two of the rustlers had taken positions behind the dirt mound of the root cellar. The other was hidden behind the well.

Luke slid out of the saddle and slipped up behind the outlaw at the well. The man's attention was focused on the frontal attack. He was firing a rifle as rapidly as he could cock it and squeeze the trigger. Luke grabbed his .44 and brought the butt of it down on the outlaw's head. He dropped the rifle and fell backward. The other two were some distance away and didn't notice the lessening of gunfire.

Luke moved in closer to them. "Drop your guns!" he yelled.

One of them did as he was told. The other turned quickly, gun in hand, eager to pump lead into Luke. Luke fired first. The outlaw's bullet plowed harmlessly through the dirt as he fell.

"Hold your fire!" he shouted. "We've got 'em."

It turned out that the man Luke shot was the one who'd killed his two partners. According to the outlaw who surrendered, he was also the one who'd forced Hatch to tell about the loot Lange had hidden away. Hatch had told them that Lange was going to meet him at the ranch. The outlaw had shot Hatch then, and the five of them were waiting for Lange to show up so they could force him to reveal his hiding place.

"Can't say I feel much sympathy for the fellow," said Fahl, referring to Hatch. "He was involved in almost everything that happened."

The posse buried the three dead outlaws and took the other two to Braxton. As far as Luke was concerned, his assignment was finished. He could return to Denver and to his son—at least for a while.

In spite of everything, there was an air of celebration when they arrived back in town that night.

Let them celebrate, thought Luke. All he wanted was a bath and a nice clean bed.

"I'm riding on out to tell the boss what happened to Ham," said Fahl. "I'll bring your mule back when I come."

"I'm leaving too," said Charlie. "They'll all be anxious for news at the ranch. I'll tell Bledsoe it's safe for him to return and open his store. I don't think anybody who knows about his trouble in Kansas is going to want to ship him back."

"I expect you're right," Luke agreed. "Tell him to come on and get busy with his dust rag."

Charlie chuckled. "Knowing him, I expect that's the first thing he'll do."

The following morning when Luke arrived at the café, clean shaven and rested, there was a bunch of towns-people there to greet him.

"We had a meeting last night," said Peacock. "I'm now

the mayor until a proper election can be held. Sinclair has agreed to serve as a council member, and so has Barney Odem, who is our new undertaker. We've drafted Coffer too. Dr. Vanhelden has the remaining council seat."

"Sounds like you've made some good choices," said Luke, who couldn't help but notice that Lily was beaming. In a fresh gingham dress, she looked prettier than ever.

"We have another choice to make," said Peacock. "We need a lawman, a real lawman. We want you, Cochran. Now, we can't pay what they pay you up in Denver, but the city has confiscated Lange's house, and it's yours if you take the job."

"Please take it, Luke," said Lily. "This town needs you."

Luke thought about his son and his sister-in-law and her husband. Maybe this was his chance to keep Gareth close, his chance to be an important part of the boy's life.

"Can I hire a deputy?" he asked.

"Sure you can," said Peacock.

"Then I'll take the job. My brother-in-law has worked as a deputy a time or two, and I want to move him and my sister-in-law down here, along with my son, Gareth."

"That house is sure big enough for all of you," said Peacock. "We'll be glad to welcome your kin to Braxton, Marshal. Only now you're going to be a town marshal instead of a deputy U.S. marshal. Guess that must seem like a step down."

Not to Luke, it didn't.

After the impromptu meeting, he had the luxury of eating a well-earned breakfast in peace.

"I can't wait to meet your family," said Lily, bringing him his second cup of coffee.

Her smile lit up the whole room. It was a smile he would have missed if he'd gone back to Denver. Now he was going to be able to see that smile anytime he wanted.

"You'll meet my family soon," he replied. "It won't be long now."

03/08/12